S0-ADY-086

"*The Fan Man* cuts through so many games that it leaves a trail of clear light." —Ram Dass

"This short, artfully structured, supremely insane novel is Buddha's story, turned inside out. . . . Horse Badorties walks into American literature a full-blown achievement, a heroic godheaded head, a splendid creep, a sublime prince of the holy trash pile." —William Kennedy, *New Republic*

"Old Horse is one hell of a character, man."
—*Philadelphia Bulletin*

"[*The Fan Man*] is a delightfully, often devastatingly funny novel. . . . William Kotzwinkle is a first-rate fabulist and has created in Horse Badorties a new kind of American character who, while dwelling in the realms of the fantastic, touches upon far more aspects of contemporary life than do many so-called American characters."
—*Seattle Times*

"Kotzwinkle has invented a human dada, full of one-line gags and comic perceptions."
—*The New York Times Book Review*

"Kotzwinkle's story of a drug-flavored, flailing genius is a fine and funny piece of work that deserves to outlive many more studious efforts to limn the psychedelic ethos—and to wind up, perhaps, in some college lit class of the future, along with Thompson and Wolfe, all examples of a rare and exotic strain of experience that crept into the literature of the sixties and seventies." —*Rolling Stone*

Obelisk

Also by William Kotzwinkle

Jack in the Box
Herr Nightingale and the Satin Woman
Elephant Bangs Train
Hermes 3000
Fata Morgana
Doctor Rat
Swimmer in the Secret Sea
E.T. The Extra-Terrestrial
E.T. The Book of the Green Planet
Christmas at Fontaine's
Queen of Swords
Great World Circus
Seduction in Berlin
Jewel of the Moon
The Exile

WILLIAM KOTZWINKLE

The FAN MAN

A Dutton Obelisk Paperback

E. P. DUTTON / NEW YORK

This paperback edition of The Fan Man
first published in 1987 by E. P. Dutton.

Copyright © 1974 by William Kotzwinkle

All rights reserved. Printed in the U.S.A.

Publisher's Note: *This novel is a work of fiction. Names, characters, places, and incidents either are the product of the author's imagination or are used fictitiously, and any resemblance to actual persons, living or dead, events, or locales is entirely coincidental.*

No part of this publication may be reproduced or transmitted in any form or by any means, electronic or mechanical, including photocopy, recording, or any information storage and retrieval system now known or to be invented, without permission in writing from the publisher, except by a reviewer who wishes to quote brief passages in connection with a review written for inclusion in a magazine, newspaper, or broadcast.

Published in the United States by E. P. Dutton,
a division of NAL Penguin Inc.,
2 Park Avenue, New York, N.Y. 10016.

Published simultaneously in Canada
by Fitzhenry and Whiteside Limited, Toronto.

Library of Congress Catalog Card Number: 87-70117

ISBN: 0-525-48307-1

COBE

A portion of this book was originally published in Esquire *magazine.*

The FAN MAN

1
Horse Badorties' Number One Pad

I am all alone in my pad, man, my piled-up-to-the-ceiling-with-junk pad. Piled with sheet music, with piles of garbage bags bursting with rubbish and encrusted frying pans piled on the floor, embedded with unnameable flecks of putrified wretchedness in grease. My pad, man, my own little Lower East Side Horse Badorties pad.

I just woke up, man. Horse Badorties just woke up and is crawling around in the sea of abominated filthiness, man, which he calls home. Walking through the rooms of my pad, man, through broken glass and piles of filthy clothes from which I shall select my wardrobe for the day. Here, stuffed in a trash basket, is a pair of incredibly wrinkled-up muck-pants. And here, man, beneath a pile of wet newspapers is a shirt, man, with one sleeve. All I need now, man, is a tie, and here is a perfectly good rubber Japanese toy snake, man, which I can easily form into an acceptable knot looking like a gnarled ball of spaghetti.

SPAGHETTI! MAN! Now I remember. That is why I have arisen from my cesspool bed, man, because of the growlings of my stomach. It is time for breakfast, man. But first I must make a telephone call to Alaska.

Must find telephone. Important deal in the making. Looking around for telephone, fighting my way through piles of sheet music, man, piled up to the ceiling. And here is an electric extension cord, man, which will serve perfectly as a belt to hold up my falling-down Horse Badorties pants, simply by running the cord through the belt loops and plugging it together.

Looking through the shambles wreckage busted chair old sardine can with a roach in it, empty piña-colada bottle, sweet sticky gummy something on the wall, broken egg on the floor, some kind of coffee grounds sprinkled around. What's this under here, man?

It's the sink, man. I have found the sink. I'd recognize it anywhere . . . wait a second, man . . . it is not the sink but my Horse Badorties big stuffed easychair piled with dirty dishes. I must sit down here and rest, man, I'm so tired from getting out of bed. Throw dishes onto the floor, crash break shatter. Sink down into the damp cushions, some kind of fungus on the armrest, possibility of smoking it.

I'm in my little Horse Badorties pad, man, looking around. It's the nicest pad I ever had, man, and I'm getting another one just like it down the hall. Two pads, man. The rent will be high but it's not so bad if you don't pay it. And with two pads, man, I will have room to rehearse the Love Chorus, man, and we will sing our holy music and record it on my battery-powered portable falling-apart Japanese tape recorder with the corroded worn-out batteries, man, and when we play it back and listen to it we will not be able to hear it. How wonderful, man.

Sitting in chair, staring at wall, where paint is peeling off and jelly is dripping and hundreds of telephone numbers are written. I must make a telephone call immediately, man, that is a MUST.

Sitting in chair, staring at wall. Unable to move, man, feeling the dark heavy curtain of impassable numbness settling on me, man. Roach crawling up the wall. Yes, man, even my roaches have roaches.

Falling back to sleep, head nodding down to chest, arm falling off side of chair, fingers touching smooth plastic. I've found the phone, man. It was right beside me all the time, man, like a good little animal, and I am holding it up, man, and there is margarine in the dial holes. This, man, is definitely my telephone. My avenue of communication is now Ma Bell into whom I am inserting my dial finger, man, again and again. She's excited, man, she's responding. . . .

". . . hello? . . . hello, man, this is Horse Badorties . . . right, man, I'm putting together a little deal, man. Acapulco artichoke hearts, man, lovely stuff . . . came across the Colorado River on a raft, man, it's a little damp, but other than that . . . can you hold on a second, man, I think I hear somebody trying to break through the window."

I cannot speak a moment longer, man, without something to eat. I am weak from hunger, man, and must hunt for my refrigerator through sucked oranges, dead wood, old iron, scum-peel. Here it is, man, with the garbage-table wedged tightly against it. Tip the table, man, this is no time for formalities, I'm starving.

Some kind of mysterious vegetable, man, is sitting in the refrigerator, shriveled, filthy, covered with fungus, a rotten something, man, and it is my breakfast.

Rather than eat it, man, I will return to my bed of pain. I will reenter the Bardo of Dreams, man, if I can locate my bed. It's through this door and back in here somewhere, man. I must get some more sleep, I realize that now. I cannot function, cannot move forward, man, until I have retreated into sleep.

Crawling, man, over the bureau drawers which are bursting with old rags and my used sock collection, and slipping down, man, catching a piece of the bed, man, where I can relax upon a pile of books old pail some rocks floating around. Slipping onto my yellow smeared stiff mortified ripped wax-paper scummy sheets, man, how nice. And the last thing I do, man, before I sleep is turn on my battery-powered hand-held Japanese fan. The humming note it makes, man, the sweet and constant melodic droning lulls me to sleep, man, where I will dream symphonies, man, and wake up with a stiff neck.

2
Horse Badorties' Satchel

Horse Badorties waking up again, man. Man, what planet am I on? I seem to be contained in some weird primeval hideous grease. Wait a second, man, that is my Horse Badorties pillowcase. I am alive and well in my own Horse Badorties abominable life.

Time to get up, to get up. Get up, man, you've got to get up and go out into the day and bring fifteen-year-old chicks into your life.

I'm moving my Horse Badorties feet, man, getting my stuff together, collecting the various precious contents of my pad, man, which I MUST take along with me. I have the Japanese fan in my hand, man, and I am marching forward through my rubbish heap. Cooling myself, man, on a hot summer morning or afternoon, one of the two.

Over to the window, man, which looks far out over the rooftops to a distant tower, where the time is showing four o'clock in the afternoon. Late, man. I've got to get out of the pad or I will circle around again in it, uncovering lost treasures of ancient civilizations, and I will get hung-up and stuck here all day.

Here is my satchel, man. Now I must stuff it with essential items for survival on the street: sheet music, fan, alarm clock, tape recorder. The only final and further object which must be packed in my survival satchel is the Commander Schmuck Korean earflap cap in case I happen to hear Puerto Rican music along the way.

There are countless thousands of other things in these rooms, man, I should take along with me, in case of emergency, and since it is summertime, I MUST take my overcoat. I have a powerful intuition it will come in handy.

Many other things, man, would I like to jam in my satchel. All of it, man, I want to take it all with me, and that is why I must, after getting a last drink of water, get out of here.

Roaches scurrying over the gigantic pile of caked and stuck-together greasy dishes in my Horse Badorties sink. The water is not yet cold enough. I'm going to let the water run here, man, for a second, while it gets cold. Don't let me forget to turn it off.

I've got everything I need, man. Everything I could possibly want for a few hours on the street is already irrevocably contained in my satchel. If it gets much heavier, man, I won't be able to carry it.

"I'm turning on the tape recorder, man, to record the sound of the door closing as I go out of my pad. That long strung-out creaking noise, man, is the wonderful sound of freedom for Horse Badorties. It is the sound of liberation, man, from my compulsion to delay over and over again my departure . . . wait just a second, man, I forgot to make sure if there's one last thing I wanted to take."

Back into pad once more, man, goes the insane one in his folly. Did I forget to do anything, take anything? There is just one thing and that is to change my shoes, man, removing these plastic Japanese shoes which kill my feet, because here, man, is a Chinese gum-rubber canvas shoe for easy Horse Badorties walking. Where is the other one, man? Here it is, man, with some kind of soggy wet beans, man, sprouting inside it. I can't disturb nature's harmony, man, I'll have to wear two different shoes, man, one yellow plastic Japanese, the other red canvas Chinese, and my walking, man, will be hopelessly unbalanced. I'd better not go out at all, man.

Look, man, you have to go out. Once you go outside, man, you can always buy a fresh pair of Lower-East-Side-Ukrainian cardboard bedroom slippers which fall apart after walking half a block. Of course, man, it's quite simple when looked at rationally. Let's go, man, out the door; everything is cool.

Out the door again, man, and down the steps, down the steps, down . . . one . . . two . . . three flights of stairs. . . .

Jesus, man, I forgot my walkie-talkies. I've gone down three flights of steps, man. And I am turning around and going back up them again.

I am climbing back up the stairs because, though I am tired and falling-apart, I cannot be without my walkie-talkies, man. Common sense, man, must rule over bodily fatigue.

"It is miraculous, man. I am making a special tape-recorded announcement of this miracle, man, so that I will never forget this moment of superb unconscious intuition. Ostensibly, man, I returned for my walkie-talkies, but actually it was my unconscious mind luring me back, man, because I left the door to my pad wide fucking open. Anyone might have stepped in and carried away the valuable precious contents of my pad, man. And so I am back in the scrap-heap, man, the wretched tumbled-down strewn-about fucked-up-everything of my pad, man, and I am seeing a further miracle, man. It is the miracle of the water in the sink, man, which I left running. Man, do you realize that if I had not returned here for my walkie-talkies, I would have flooded the pad, creating tidal waves among my roaches, and also on the roaches who live downstairs with the twenty-six Puerto Rican chickens? A catastrophe has been averted, man. And what is more, now the water is almost cold, man. It just needs to run a few more minutes, man, and I can have my drink of water."

But first, man, I see that I forgot to take my sweet little moon-lute, man, hanging here inside the stove. The moon-lute, man, the weirdest fucking instrument on earth, man. Looks like a Chinese frying pan, man, and I am the only one in the occidental world who would dare to play it, man, as it sounds like a Chinaman falling down a flight of stairs. Which reminds me, man, I'd better get out of this pad, man, and down the stairs. I'm going, man, I'm on the way, out of the door. I am closing up the pad, man, without further notice.

3
Horse Badorties' Bottle of Piña-Colada

The street, man, dig the street. I'm free of my pad, man. I'm out here in a summer day walking along carrying satchel and overcoat. Man, why did I bring this overcoat I must take it back to my Horse Badorties pad immediately.

"This is Horse Badorties turning on the tape recorder, man, collecting more valuable sounds. Dig, man, the hum in the background. Horse Badorties is flaked out in the

Clear White Grease, man, standing in front of the great Con Edison power transformer. Dig, man, the loud humming dragon, man, listen to it. I wish I could stay and listen to it, man, but I've got to recruit fifteen-year-old chicks for the Love Chorus, man, IMMEDIATELY!"

Horse Badorties turning onto Avenue A, man, what a wonderful street. Look at the filth, man, everywhere. It's my pad, man, Avenue A is merely an extension of my ever-shifting shitpile. Why, man, did I bring this overcoat with me? It must be ninety degrees in the shade of a New York TREE!

"Tree, man . . . this is Horse Badorties, man, turning on the tape recorder, to announce The Plan, man. It is this, I am remembering a certain tree, man, in Van Cortlandt Park where I grew up as a child. And that, man, THAT is where we are going, man, on a holy pilgrimage to Van Cortlandt Park, where as a little kid, I spaced myself out. Let's go, man, IMMEDIATELY!"

The thought of this forgotten childhood park is now acting upon my Horse Badorties mind. There are some five hundred other things I must do in the meantime—hustle fans, hustle chicks, hustle music—and all these things are imperative and not to be set aside for a moment. But think of it, man, in spite of all the things you have to do, the trees of Van Cortlandt Park, growing free and green and covered with soot. I must go there at once.

First, however, I must go to Tompkins Square Park, where run-away fifteen-year-old chicks are undoubtedly congregating. First, however, I must fan myself, cool myself with my hand-held battery-driven fan before I drop of heat prostration carrying this motherfucking overcoat. Cool breezes, man, across my brow.

The reason I haven't gone into Chinese paper fans, man, is because I haven't been to Chinatown lately, but I must go there TONIGHT. Put it on tape, man, so you don't forget it. "We're going to Chinatown for dinner, man. It's in The Plan. Don't let me forget it, will you?" The Plan is now formulated on my Horse Badorties tape recorder. Later on, when I have forgotten who I am, I can always turn on the tape recorder and find out that I am Horse Badorties, going to Chinatown. And now, man, I must get out of this doorway and walk along the street.

There is a Horse Badorties footstep, man, and there is another one. I am crossing the street successfully, man, but hold everything, STOP! I hear Puerto Rican music, man.

Quickly digging out of the Horse Badorties survival satchel the Commander Schmuck Imperial Red Chinese Army hat, man, I am putting it on my head, and lowering the thick pile-stuffed earflaps over my ears, man, closing off the sound of Puerto Rican gourd players singing

muy bonita
mi corazón

I can still hear faint strains of it, man, but I am walking away fast. The Commander Schmuck hat has saved my eardrums again, man, from an onslaught worse than

Ukrainian folk-songs. My Commander Schmuck hat is a winter hat, and though it is summertime, I am wearing it into Tompkins Square Park, and now, man, NOW I see why.

At last, man, I know why I brought this overcoat with me. In order not to draw attention to the unusual presence of the Commander Schmuck Imperial Winter Hat with anti-Puerto-Rican-music earflaps, man, which might attract the eye of a wandering policeman, I am putting on the winter overcoat, man, so that the cop, seeing me in winter hat and overcoat will notice only that my wardrobe is complete. And by the time he realizes something is amiss, man, I will have completely melted out of sight into a small puddle of sweat on the sidewalk. And now, man, I see chicks walking around in Tompkins Square Park.

"Hey, baby, here's a piece of sheet music for you. Hang onto it all day and bring it with you tonight to St. Nancy's Church on the Bowery. Sing this music, baby, and be filled with thrill-vibrations."

"Oh, I can't read music."

"This music is waiting for you, baby, just below the surface of your waking mind. By coming to St. Nancy's Church tonight at eight o'clock you will be taking the rapid upward path to instant musicianship. After rehearsal, Maestro Badorties will give you a private lesson at his Fourth Street Music Academy, above the Puerto Rican grocery store where, with unlimited credit he and his staff have purchased party sandwiches and will be brewing select teas from brightly painted tins in the Academy kitchen. Look at this music all day, baby . . . I'll see you tonight. . . ."

"Can I bring a friend?"

"The Academy opens its arms to all students under the age of sixteen, who are given special scholarships, including her own room. We are presently negotiating with the landlord for the entire top floor of the building. Sing it tonight, baby, and bring your friends."

I feel like I'm passing out, man. Too much exertion of the precious contents of my energies inside this fifty-pound black overcoat. I've got to get some food, man, or I will pass out. Get out of this park, man, and go to a grocery store, QUICK, and get a bottle of piña-colada soft drink. As a four-star general in the Puerto Rican Liberation Forces, man, Commander Schmuck is entitled to one bottle a day.

But first I had better stop in the drug store, man, and buy an astrology book for this month, to find out what's happening to me, man. Because something must be happening, man.

"What's happening, man." Smack fifty cents down on drugstore counter and walk off with my Horse Badorties genuine Aries natal program starbook, for today, let's see:

A mixed or muddled order
and chaos threatens.

Another wonderful average Horse Badorties day, man.

I'm mixed, muddled, and don't know where I'm going. I'd better rewind my tape recorder, man, and find out where I'm going. Because right now I'm standing on a street corner, going nowhere.

Little wheels of tape recorder spinning around. Click *on* button, hear:

"Chinatown for dinner, man. It's in The Plan."

"Right, man, I dig." Horse Badorties is completely oriented now. Chinatown. The only question is: Chinatown in San Francisco or New York City? I could catch a plane to Frisco and be there by morning. Here is a chick, man, another chick who wants to sing.

"Hey, baby, dig this music . . . tonight . . . St. Nancy's on the Bowery. . . ."

The thing, man, that holds me together is my MISSION, man, for chicks and music. Without that, man, I am an empty bottle of piña-colada, which is what I must do immediately, man, enter my local Puerto Rican grocery store and empty a bottle of piña-colada.

"May I halp you?" On a shelf over the head of the grocery lady, man, is a radio, and even through the Commander Schmuck earflaps, man, I hear the insufferable chicken-rhythms of Puerto Rican music. It's too much, man. I'll have to get out of here and skip the bottle of piña-colada.

4
A Knight of the Hot Dog

I am going downtown toward Chinatown, man. What a lovely day for a long walk twenty or thirty blocks down to Chinatown. I better take a subway, man.

Going down the subway steps the oh no man dark subway steps down into the subway. Why, man, am I going down into the subway when I could be up in the fresh air? Here comes the Japanese No-play again, man: I'm moving in the slowest possible way, man, like a slow-motion dream, on the landing between the sidewalk above and the subway below, wondering, man, in my own hopelessly compulsive Horse Badorties way, what is the best thing to do with the day? I know of only one solution, man, and that is my fan.

Digging into satchel and withdrawing fan. Turning on the little blades, man, and the warm air is blown against my face and I am alive again, man, in the humming breezes.

Blue-haired old lady going down the steps. She needs a fan, man. Walk down beside her and cool her with gentle air currents.

"What a lovely breeze."

"Yes, ma'n. Everyone needs a Horse Badorties fan. Take it with you on the subway and never be oppressed. Special buy-of-a-lifetime today, only $1.95. I wish I could sell you this one, but it's my only sample. Pick one up sometime."

"I must do that. It's so cool."

Going through the turnstile, man, clak-a-cruntcha through the turnstile, and into the dark tunnel. Lunatics everywhere. Happily I am fanning myself and wearing an overcoat so as not to be mistaken for a lunatic. I'm in the subway, man. What, man, am I doing in the subway? Here comes the train, I can feel the wind against my face, the great vacuum fan, pushing the air along ahead of it, rippling my beard. There is the subway driver, man, in his little control room, looking out the window. I salute him with my fan, man, and now I am getting in the subway car and am actually going to Chinatown when I should be going to Van Cortlandt Park to climb through the bushes. I was born up there, man. And soon I will return there to walk in the grass and have dreams, man!

Directly across from me, man, is the subway window. And since it is dark in the tunnel and lighted in the subway car, I can see my Horse Badorties head reflected with hair sticking out in ninety different directions. Weird-looking Horse Badorties. Horse Badorties making demon little ratty face, crawling eyeballs into corners, wrinkling nose up rodentlike, pulling gums back, sticking teeth out, making slow chewing movements. Freaking myself out, man, and several other people in the car.

Fanning myself with plastic breezes, making weird faces, what else, man, is needed? Only one other thing, man, and that is a tremendously deep and resonant Horse Badorties Tibetan lama bass note which he is now going to make:

"Braaaaaaaaaaaaaaauuuuuuuuuuuuuuuummmmmmmmmmmmmmnnnnnnnnnnn."

Mothers with their children look at me, man, and then explain to their kiddies that if you don't learn to blow silent farts in church you will turn out like that awful man. But the kids know, man, they know it is better to freely release the energies.

However, while other passengers are sweltering in the summer heat, Horse Badorties swelters twice as much because he is wearing an overcoat. Subway doors opening see sign says

CANAL STREET

must get satchel closed this is my Horse Badorties stop.

"HOLD THE DOORS, MAN!" Putting away fan, trying to stand up, trying to get moving in gigantic overcoat, moving toward doors, which are closing on my Horse Badorties beard, entrapping the hairs and forcing me to stand here, man, without moving lest I receive the exquisite pain, man, of tearing out my beard by the roots.

I am going an extra stop, man, with my beard caught in the door, so I can approach Chinatown from ten or fifteen blocks below. To stimulate the appetite, man.

Here is the next stop, man, my beard is released and I am going out of the car and up the steps, man, coming out among the many warehouses below Chinatown. Streets are empty. The workday is over. Horse Badorties is completely alone, man, and in that case, it is time to step into a doorway.

Open satchel take out special Montgomery Ward mail-order glass-enclosed water-filled wire-screened rubber-hosed lung-preserving mother-fucking hookah. And out of my moisture-proof herbalist's pouch I am removing a generous pinch of Mexican papaya leaf, man, to get my enzymes flowing, sprinkling the leaves into the bowl of the hookah. And then I dig out the World's Fair award-winning best-design Japanese perpetual match—a small square metal container filled with lighter fluid, in which a slender steel-supported wick of flint and cotton is immersed. By simply pulling out this match of cotton-steel and striking it along the abrasive face of the container, I shall have fire with which to light my health-food pipe.

Scratch . . . scratch

It doesn't seem to be working, man. The Japanese perpetual match is temporarily on the blink, man, and I am reverting back to old-style book-matches, and have ignition. I have lift-off, man, I am inhaling the smoke and rising, man, all four burners on in my brain. The big bird is afloat, man.

Yes, man, there is nothing like health-food smoke from herbs grown by Mexican monks in their jungle monasteries. Good for bent mind, scaly elbows, and the purple dorkies.

The big bird is floating toward Chinatown, man, to the mysterious land of tree ears and fried rice. Good wholesome macrobiotic vegetarian food. But first, man, I must buy a HOT DOG from this hot dog wagon on the street.

But first, man, I must buy the hot dog seller's gigantic umbrella.

"How much you want for the umbrella, man?"

"Umbrella not for sale. You want hot dog, mustard, sauerkraut?"

"I want this umbrella, man, this enormous red white and blue umbrella with the hot dog pictured on the side of it, man, how much do you want for it?"

"Not for sale."

"Ten bucks, man, cash."

"It don't belong to me, it belongs the company."

"Dig, man, you tell the motherfucking company that the wind blew it down the street and a Puerto Rican kid grabbed it and ran off into a doorway and you couldn't follow him or his gang would steal your little truck too. What's a hot dog salesman supposed to do for the company, man, beat off attackers with a rubber hot dog? Come on, man, don't be a sap."

Hippie wise guy takin hold of the numbrella, why not let him steal it. He gives me ten bucks, he steals it. Somebody stole the umbrella, just like he said. Right, he stole, yeah. "All right, gimme the ten."

"You're a true corporate structure man, man. Help me roll this thing up."

Rolling up the red white and blue umbrella along the shaft.

"OK, scram outa here."

"If it rains, man, if it rains." I'm covered, man, all the way. Walking along, man, carrying an incredible umbrella, man, big as a fucking flag pole. It's heavy, man. Practically breaking my arm to carry. I'm so happy, man, to have this umbrella with my insignia on it of crossed hot dogs on a bun.

Many fifteen-year-old chicks in a rainstorm can fit under this umbrella with Horse Badorties. An auspicious purchase, man, I'd better check my horoscope.

A journey will turn out more expensive than you bargained for.

Right, man, I bought a fucking ten dollar umbrella, and am carrying it up through the backstreets into Chinatown, man, where all the stoned-out Chinamen are sitting on their doorsteps, man, tripping on ginseng root and salt-plums.

"This is Horse Badorties, man, tape recording a message for the great time capsule to be buried in concrete and dug up tomorrow. I'm in Chinatown, man, and I am receiving brain flashes from previous lifetimes as a Chinaman, man. Used to play Chinese flute, man, a thousand years ago, under a doorstep. Yes, man, I used to be in the court of the Paper Dragon, and speaking of dragging, man, my right arm is scraping along the ground from all the satchel, fan, and heavy umbrella I'm carrying around. It is time, man, to go into this little Chinese store and buy more stuff, man, to make my trip even heavier."

Chinese toys, man. Little wooden people in a rowboat, a miniature tea-set, a toy drum, buy, buy, buy. . . .

Thank goodness I am out of that little store, man, having bought only fifteen precious valuable worthless objects. And dig, man, here comes a fifteen-year-old Chinese chick, man, with beautiful eyes and long black hair. Man, how I would love to bowl in her pagoda.

"Here, baby, dig this music." Hand special sheet music to almond-eyed smiling turned-on Chinese chick. "Sing it tonight, baby, at St. Nancy's Church on the Bowery. As you see we have included the Chinese drum in our ensemble." Take out toy drum, give to chick. "Here, baby, take this drum, carry it around, bang when you feel like it, and come to St. Nancy's eight o'clock tonight, the address is on that sheet of music. I'd like to say more, but I must get some other plastic assorted instruments, wander around, fall down, have dinner, and get lost. Come to St. Nancy's, baby, and we'll roll the *I Ching* together. See you later, baby, later."

Here is a little tin sword, man, cheap enough, suitable for a four-star general in the Puerto Rican cavalry, riding a giant roach.

It's time to get out of Chinatown, man, as I'm in a fit of wild buying. But first I must purchase this pair of black chopsticks, might as well purchase three or four pairs.

Walking along, man, drawn to the store-front Buddhist temple of Kwan-yin. Must go inside, man, and get my fortune.

Old Chinese men inside, sitting on folding chairs, reading newspapers, talking, looking at nothing, spaced-out Chinamen, man.

Walk past them to the bowl of fortunes in front of the statue of Kwan-yin, beautiful goddess of good luck. Drop a quarter in the fortune bowl and draw out a little roll of paper, wrapped up in a rubber band. Tiny magic fortune scroll. Unroll it, read:

The umbrella of the Buddha opens out over you as a smile. Good fortune indeed.

Right, man, the umbrella is checking out on all sides. Destiny, man, you can't fight it. But in order to perform the heroic duty of a Knight of the Hot Dog and carry my enormous umbrella, I must have something to eat immediately, man.

Out of the temple, man, and back into the noisy street, maybe buy a few soybean curds, man, healthful, nutritious square blobular gummy-textured disgusting bean curds, man, make anyone but a Chinaman pass out from eating them.

Wait a second, man, here is a fantastic box of gray hundred-year-old eggs, man. Eat one and die instantly. "Let me have half a dozen, better make it a dozen, of these eggs, please, thank you." No more room in my satchel, man, I'll have to carry them in my overcoat.

What else, man, shall I get to eat? A salty Chinese cookie and some black-bean soup, so salty, man, you are thirsty for a week after downing some.

I'd better go up to Forty-second Street, man, and have fifteen steamed-rubber hamburgers.

5 The Overcoat That Went to the Bronx

Here is the perfect restaurant, called the Grand, man, a broken-down little cheap authentic Chinese eating place, man, where only Chinese cats eat. What a wonderful restaurant. Let's go somewhere else, man, they don't have a telephone.

"You wan' eat someting?"

"Give me some fried rice, man."

Just a little hole-in-the-wall restaurant, man, I can look

back into the kitchen where the old Chinese cook is stirring the rice around. It's hot back there, man, by the stove. "Hey, man, you need a fan. Feel the breezes, man. Straight from the Yellow River. Buy a fan, man, only one dollar and ninety-five cents, make you one with your ancestors."

Clazy Mellican boy.

"Is this my rice here, man? I'll take it out myself, save the waitress a tip."

What a beautiful dish of light fluffy rice, with tiny pieces of mushroom in it and soy sauce, man. This is the only way to eat, man, the Way of Heaven. Rice, man, a chick ate only rice over in New Jersey and she died, man, faded away. I don't know, man, fuck this rice, I'd better go down the street to the bakeshop and buy instead a huge juicy big stuffed meatbun, man.

"You no like rice?"

"I have just remember an important message waiting for me outside in a telephone booth. Would you put this rice in a container for me? Thank you so much, I must get out of here and don't forget to buy a fan if your chop suey is too hot you can cool it. So long, man!"

Put container of rice in satchel, man, and go down the street, man, to the little bake shop, and there in the window, man, are the hot fresh-stuffed buns, stuffed with ground-up cooked-up delicious dead cow, turn rotten in my guts fuck my mind up with death anxiety putrification. I can't do it, man. I am passing up the stuffed meatbun, WHICH REMINDS ME, man! It is time for the Love Chorus rehearsal and chicks will be there, man, and perhaps, man, I will stuff my meat in their buns. LET'S GO!

Back to the subway, man, and down the steps, here comes the train, man, I'll have to hurry, man, hurry, through the turnstile.

Clack-a-cruntcha

I think, man, I just broke a hundred-year-old egg inside my overcoat pocket, man.

Hurry, man, hurry, the doors to the train are still open. "HOLD THOSE DOORS, MAN!"

The conductor sees me running, man, with satchel and umbrella, he'll hold the doors, man, he'll hold them as I go through, I'm going through, man, he is closing the doors directly upon me, man.

Floppa-cracka

He got me, man, right in the pocketful of hundred-year-old eggs, man. The smell, man, coming out of those eggs, man, which have been allowed to age for an entire year. A pocketful of broken eggs, man, is too horrible. There is only one thing worse that I know of, man, and that is the time I saw a chick, man, sitting across from me in the subway, a spaced-out chick, man, squirming around kind of weirdlike, man, like she was trying to lay a hundred-year-old egg. And when the doors opened at the next stop, man, she got off in a hurry, leaving behind her on the seat, a TURD, man. And directly into the subway car in the next moment, man, comes this dude, in a brand new white raincoat, man, looking like *Esquire* magazine, man, and as the dude was in a hurry, man, he sat down without looking, directly onto the turd, man. And suddenly, man, people started moving away from him, the way they are moving away from me now, man, because of a dozen incredibly rotten eggs in my pocket. There is only one solution, man. Like the chick, I must leave a rotten deposit behind me, and slip out of this overcoat. This is my stop, man. Good-bye, little overcoat, take care of yourself.

Man, how good it feels to be free of that fucking overcoat and also, man, now I do not have to eat any hundred-year-old eggs, man, how wonderful. It is time for rehearsal, man, of the Love Chorus, so do not get hung up anywhere, proceed directly up the subway steps to St. Nancy's Church on the Bowery.

6 Fugue in A Minor

Walking up the Bowery, man, carrying satchel and umbrella, through the bums. Bums, man, falling beaten broken crutches in the doorways sleeping, man. Bums creeping fall into doorway teeth dropping out lying down among the garbage cans. There's no place like home, man, and I feel like a nap myself, but I must proceed with my mission, to get all fifteen-year-old chicks singing Love Music. And after that, man, I am going to retire to

Van Cortlandt Park and sing with the frogs at noon and midnight.

But now, man, here is St. Nancy's Church on the Bowery, and here I am once again, Maestro Badorties, walking up the stone steps—which reminds me, man—always before doing music, it is necessary to vivify the corpuscles in the brain cage with the sacred smoke of the cultured herbal leaf. Let me just go around the corner, man, into a doorway here out of the wind, and stuff my Arabian camel-saddle-pipe with carefully-processed fig leaves, the smoke of which I am now drawing deeply into my system, and which I hold there for maximum benefit. Yes, man, all my brain cells are suddenly saying, *Hello, Horse,* and I have once more the power of a spaced-out camel. Across the desert sands, man, I am creeping out of this doorway. Numerous and incredible subtleties are now appearing to me, man, of rare and extraordinary design and the one I must select and concentrate on is that one which keeps me from being struck by the Bowery Avenue BUS, watch out, man!

Alright, man, up the church steps again, to perform the musical activity for which you were born and toward which all your training leads you—the conducting of fifteen-year-old chicks to the sublime heights of song and then later, still higher, to the ethereal regions of your fourth floor pad, where you will, in your capacity as Avatar of Song, screw them puce.

"Good evening, Horse," says the priest, inside the door.

"Good evening, Father."

"All of the chorus is here, and I think I see some new faces."

"Yes, Father, I have been out recruiting more chicks and circulating leaflets in great number announcing the concert."

The Super Hot Dog Mission of Horse Badorties, man, is slowly taking shape. For an entire year, man, I have held the Love Chorus together, dragging the valuable precious contents of my body here every night for rehearsal, and now, man, we are almost ready for our first performance. All we need is twenty-five fans, and I have ordered them, man, they are on the way.

Up the aisle, man, and up the stairs to the balcony where the Love Chorus is assembled—fifteen-year-old chicks, man, whom I have trained to sing the old church music, little known to the world, never heard in modern churches, but which I have uncovered from old vaults, locked drawers, and secret hiding places of old tombs. Most Church music, man, is enough to make me ill, man, make me shriek and feel awful, depressed rotten and piled-up with gloom, so lousy is it, man, so corny and terrible, written by old ladies and sung by zombies. But this church music, man, which I have found, is the white bird of reality, man, written by old cats in the Middle Ages, man, who were locked into wondrous harmonies, man, which make my hair stand on end, and that is why my hair is always sticking out in ninety different directions.

"Good evening, everyone."

All the good little chiclets say *Good Evening, Horse.*

"I have a special announcement. Here in my hand you see a battery-powered fan, which makes a constant humming note, a drone around which we will all sing, strengthening our chords and opening our inner ear. I have ordered a fan for each of you, and we will sing, holding them in our hands. Nothing like it has ever been done before. All right, let us begin."

"But I don't know how to read music!" A new chick, just joined the Love Chorus tonight.

"Dig, baby, the notes are in your soul. Just hold this sheet music in your hand and pretty soon you'll find your way. All right, Love Chorus, places, please. From the beginning, one, two. . . ."

And we are into the music again. The new chick is spaced out, man, does not believe she can read music, but soon, man, soon the stream will carry her away, and she will dig that she knows exactly where the music is going because it couldn't go anywhere else. Dive in, baby, you wouldn't be here tonight if you didn't already know all about music. She's here, man, in the broken-down church in the fucked-up East Village because her soul said, go. The soul knows, man, and old Maestro Horse Badorties goes straight to the soul every time. It's no good, man, trying to teach music, the only way is to push the chick right into her soul-stream, man, where she'll learn immediately.

She's opening her mouth, man, she is making a musical note, there she is, man, I can see it lighting up her face. Instant recognition: *I know this music.* Smile. Spontaneous rapture of childhood recaptured. Another member of the Love Chorus has just been reborn, man. The ear hears, the heart knows, the voice sings out. You don't need music school, baby, you've got it made.

Maestro Badorties keeps the Love Chorus together, man, in supreme polyphonic harmony. This music, man, is from the angel of radiant joy in the central realm of the densely-packed, and when it is done right, it elevates my hot dog soul to the region of ecstasy. And it will sound a thousand times better, man, when everyone has a fan.

"Very good, that was terrible, the worst singing I ever heard except for one of two moments which were magnificent beyond belief. We will all meet again tomorrow night. Should for any reason I be retained, derailed, or deported, you all know how to continue practicing. Since this is the greatest music ever written, you will have no trouble. Father, we are all thankful to you for this wonderful church you gave us again tonight as a meeting place, see you tomorrow night."

"It sounded wonderful," says Father.

"Yes, it was terrible, and it will be even worse in time for our concert, unless my fans arrive, which are guaranteed to keep us resonating perfectly." And now down the little winding steps of the balcony and out of the church into the night.

And standing on the street, man, is the beautiful Chinese chick, smiling.

"I listened to the music. It sounded beautiful."

"Dig, baby, it will sound even better when we go back to my Fourth Street Academy pad and hear it played back at the wrong speed inside this worn-out tape recorder. Come on, baby, I'll give you a lesson in sight-reading."

Quietly giving her delicate oriental assent to my suggestion, the Chinese chick walks beside me, man, through the picturesque Lower East Side streets, lined with wet thrown-out couches, on which little children are playing, jumping on the springs and sailing through the air.

"It's right here, baby, through this door falling off the hinges, and up the steps. . . ." A beautiful Chinese chick, man, returning with me to my Horse Badorties pad. In a few moments she will be experiencing the wonder of instantaneous sight-reading ability through the special Maestro Badorties thought-transference sex intercourse copulation fucky technique. "Wait a second, baby, wait right here on this landing. I must run down to the store and get a box of teaballs, it'll only take two minutes." Going down the steps, taking two at a time, as teaballs are a must, man, to simulate the oriental environment.

"Good ebening."

"Two bottles of piña-colada to go, man . . . open the bottles, please, thank you. . . ."

"Twenty-fi' cen', please."

"All you need, man, is a fan to keep your bananas cool.

Dig, man, the breeze from this little Japanese . . . EX-CUSE ME, MAN, I have just remember an important engagement on the stairs . . . so long, man!" Go back up the steps quickly, man, overcoming the tendency to forget the main object at hand, which in this case is a Chinese chick on whom I must get my hands. There she is, man, still smiling, waiting for her music lesson.

"OK, baby, I've got the all-important piña-colada, and there are just two more flights to go to the top of the building."

And up we go to the fourth floor, man, to where my wonderful Horse Badorties pad is located. How very odd, man. Someone seems to have clamped a huge padlock on the door to my pad.

"This is the work of the landlord, baby. He's trying to keep burglars out. See, here in the lock is a note explaining everything. It is in the form of an eviction notice, to make burglars think all the contents of the pad have been moved out."

By merely taking out of my Horse Badorties survival satchel a handy ball-peen hammer, with one powerful blow of the tool, man, I have smashed the lock open.

"All right, baby, everything is in order now, step right through. As you can clearly see, the valuable precious contents of the pad have not been stolen."

The pad, man. Incredible mountains of objects of moldy fig newtons and tuna fish cans confronting us, man, blurring the vision, fucking the mind up. How wonderful, man, to be home again. Man, I left the water running in the sink.

"Look at that water running all over the place, baby, flooding the pad, there must be a foot of water over everything, and dig, baby, this water is now COLD ENOUGH TO DRINK! If you were me, would you drink this filthy poisoned recirculated shit-water?"

"Is this where you live?"

"This is my study. You'll notice I am studying action painting, throwing modern art objects here and there, tin cans, paper bags. Don't step on anything if you can help it, it is all arranged according to number."

"Jesus, you have a lot of stuff here."

"It is a lifetime's work. If only I could get a frame around that splash of colored grease on the wall, mixed with old tomato paste. Do you think I should knock the whole wall down and take it to the Museum of Modern Art in my school bus?"

"I think you should shut off the water."

"You're right, baby, there is no point in drinking this New York City water when we have in our hands a bottle each of piña-colada, the Puerto Rican soft drink to make your teeth fall out. And maybe we can find something to eat on the floor. . . . WAIT A SECOND, MAN! I'VE GOT IT!" In my satchel, man, waiting there for me, synchronistically planned by my unconscious mind to coordinate with my meeting this Chinese chick is a long-forgotten but perfectly intact two containers of . . .

"Fried rice, baby, dig, and some chopsticks."

I have scored, man, I have wigged the chick with fried rice. We were meant for each other, man, she knows it, I know it, we're happy with fried rice, if only we had a juicy steak to go with it.

And now, man, that we have eaten and drunk, there is the undeniable presence in my pants of a Horse Badorties hard-on. It has been such a long time, man, since I had time to fuck a chick, and here she is, man, smiling at me, giving me the fifteen-year-old power-wave of just awakened sexuality. I am going to her, going slowly over to where she is sitting on the arm of my stuffed chair, and I run my fingers through her jet-black hair and she turns her head up to me, man, her lips, eyes, the moment, man, has come, to make just one telephone call which I cannot postpone a moment longer.

"Just a second, baby, while we digest our rice I have just remembered to call my printer, who is working the night shift turning out thousands of sheets of publicity for the Love Concert."

Here is the telephone, man, right by her foot, her little delicate oriental foot, which I caress with my sensitized dialing finger . . . dial . . . dial . . . dial.

"Hello, man, this is Horse Badorties, how's it going . . . great, man, run through another 5000 sheets . . . I'll be in tomorrow with a school bus to pick it all up . . . right, man, and listen, there's just one more thing, man . . . hold on a moment, man . . . hold on . . . I. . . ." Have to touch this chick, man, run my hand up her legs, man, lift her skirt up to her black Chinese underwear with red dragons on it. Man, I must get a shipload of this underwear to give out with fans to the entire CHORUS!

"Where can I lay my skirt, I don't want to get it all greasy."

"There must be a spot around here somewhere, baby . . . I don't know . . . you better keep it under your arm."

"Take that scratchy old jacket off," she says, playfully removing my jacket.

"Be careful where you lay that jacket down, baby. I might not be able to find it again."

We struggle around in the junk, man, trying to find a place to lay down, but it is not safe on the floor, even the roaches are going around in little paper boats. "We'll have to do it standing up, baby."

She reaches for my Horse Badorties pants, man, and I am knocked off balance, and we topple, down into the unknown impossible-to-describe trash pile. We are rolling around in the dark contents—old loaf of bread, bicycle tire, bunch of string in peanut oil, bumping weird greasy things and slimey feelings and sand and water, lid of a tin can floating by on a sponge. There's my book on telepathy with a roach on page twelve reading about the Dalai Lama. I cannot get my prick into the chick yet, man, as I have just remembered another phone call which I must make, man. It should be made now, man, because one thing I don't dig is *coitus interruptus*, so I'd better make the call before we officially begin balling.

"This will just take a minute, baby, I have to call a junkyard in New Jersey, the owner is waiting for me to confirm a school bus, just relax, baby, while I dial."

Direct dialing, man, straight to the junkyard. My complicated life, man. There are so many things to handle at once when you are head of the Fourth Street Music Academy and must purchase a school bus to carry fifteen-year-old chicks around in, from state to state. We're going to live in that school bus, man, and put beds in it and a washing machine.

"Hello? . . . hello, Mr. Thorne, how are you doing, man. . .   This is Horse Badorties in New York City . . . yes, man, right . . . I wanted to tell you I will be over tomorrow to purchase the school bus, so please don't sell it to any other traveling artist. Yes, I'll be there about noontime . . . right . . . so long, man. . . ."

"Maybe if we go in the other room," says the chick, "we could find a place to lay down."

Possibly she is right, man, and so we fight our way across the abominable sea of trash . . . abominable, man, wait a second. "Dig, baby, there is my rented typewriter, right there, under that pile of used noodles, and dig, baby, I am going to write an article IMMEDIATELY for *Argosy* magazine about an enormous footprint found in Central Asia."

"There's even more junk in this room," she says, looking into my Horse Badorties bedroom.

"Right, baby, but if we crawled up on top of these

boxes of sheet music we could perform a fugue, come on, baby, let's try."

It is the perfect place to screw, man, because it is better than a music lesson, the chick will assimilate directly through her ass cheeks the music of the Love Chorus.

"That's it, baby, just crawl up there, I'm right behind you."

Crawling up from box to box, man, up to a platform of other boxes stuffed with sheet music, and now, man, NOW, high above the wet filthy floor, in our heavenly tower of sheet music, this fifteen-year-old Chinese chick is giving me her sweet little meatbun.

Man, what is that ripping sound, that collapsing wet cardboard tearing sound, it is the boxes, man, falling apart below us, man, and down, man, down once again into the darkness we are falling with sheet music flying in all directions, hitting other boxes we go falling through them breaking them apart and falling further down, into the water, splash, here, man, come the roaches with a lifeboat.

All right, man, we'll just have to screw on the floor in a pile of old dishrags and a rubber overshoe. Now is the time, man, to give her the downbeat.

"I have to go," she says, standing up.

"Go? Baby, we just got here. Come on, baby, there's plenty of time."

"I have to be home by ten o'clock," she says, putting on her skirt. Fifteen-year-old chicks, man, do anything, fuck anybody, and be home by ten o'clock. I don't have the strength to protest, man, I've lost my suit jacket, I've wrecked fifteen boxes of sheet music, forgot to buy tea-balls, and as a result am not getting balled. The gods, man, arrange everything. Maybe they will arrange for her to return tomorrow night, when I have my school bus and can drive her home. Man, I'm so tired from climbing up those boxes and falling down. I've got to find my bed, man, and get some zzzzzzz's.

7
Horse Badorties Dreams

Horse Badorties having dream: Dream he is running around in a circle with elephants, hippopotamus. Teaching them to sing harmony. And here's a bear, man, riding a tricycle, carrying a hot dog umbrella.

Horse Badorties' dream: Walking up great mountain of paper bags tin cans smoking bones walking up tremendous mountain of trash. The people of the village are afraid to climb the mountain of trash because no one has ever climbed it and lived to tell the tale. Impossible maze too much piles of junk everywhere you turn. Lose balance slip sink down through old eggshells, cardboard boxes, coffee grounds, melted plastic. Man went out there up to Great Trash Mountain and was never seen again. Thousand old sardine cans in a pile flashing blinding light. Stuff everywhere to confuse you and nobody ever found their way out of it.

Horse Badorties walks up it easy. He walks up the great mountain of trash one two three, man. Horse Badorties' own backyard, that's all this Mountain of Trash is, man. Simplest thing in the world to climb climbing up up up.

Horse Badorties dreaming: Old medieval village, tell by thatched-roof cottages. Horse Badorties goes into sunlit meadow where old-type people in capes weird gowns cloaks stand together, holding precious valuable sheet music, and Horse Badorties is conducting them. Making perfect chords, Maestro Badorties is at the center of the golden meadow light with golden birds flying up in the sky.

Dream Horse Badorties: Dreaming he is in a bathtub or toilet or some kind of water-basin. A dark figure above him, pushes a screen down over him, pushing him into the water. Where's my fan, man. Horse Badorties will knock off all ugly mothers of imagination!

Horse Badorties waking up. Horse Badorties in fucking bed of pain. I'm sleeping all night in a bed of rocks, man, some kind of plastic sword in my back. What time is it, man, what universe am I in?

Horse Badorties waking up oh no not another day Horse Badorties, not another day of running around buying school bus, selling fans, going crazy. You don't want another day. Go back to sleep in your junk pile, man, catch a few more zzzzzz's. Snuggle back down into empty milk carton, valuable treasures, sink back down into. Remove wax from eardrums hear better, make small figures, start ear-wax museum. To sleep again Horse Badorties to sleep.

Horse Badorties dream he walking along and a flying saucer man is coming after him.

8 Horse Badorties' Number Two Pad

A knocking at the door, man, I have to get up and answer the door, man, stumbling falling across the room to the door.

"Yes, who is it?"

"Luke."

"Right, come on in, man," Luke, man, cat lives down the hall in the only other occupied pad on this floor. The other two pads are empty, man, and I am going to get them, soon and somehow.

"I'm going to Japan, Horse."

"You are, man? That means, man, we can get fans directly from Tokyo and eliminate the middleman, man. We can work a fantastic import-export deal, man, and not make any money."

"I'm going to enter a Buddhist monastery, Horse. No more deals."

"These fans, man, are religious objects. Half the time they don't work, man. Nirvana fans, man, perfectly motionless. Consider them on that basis and send me a hundred as soon as you get there, for distribution here among fifteen-year-old chicks."

"I don't know where the landlord is, Horse. Will you give him the key to my apartment for me?"

"Gladly, man. I would consider it a privilege to serve you in this way, seeing as you are entering the religious life."

"Thanks, Horse. Take care of yourself."

"Just answer me one question, man: That little bag you are carrying, no bigger than a gum-bag, in which only a toothbrush and safety razor could fit—is that all you are taking with you to Japan?"

"That's all, Horse."

"Incredible, man. I plan to go to Japan myself, next year, when I buy a 747 super-fortress flying boxcar, man, to take all my stuff with me, and bring fans back. I'll see you then, man, I'll see you in Japan next year, man, stay cool."

There goes Luke, man, down the steps for the last time, to a Buddhist monastery. He's on the Path, man, and so am I, directly down the hallway to his pad, man. Opening the door, and going inside. How neat, man, just like a monk's cell—bare, everything in place, only the essential objects. My new pad, man. All it needs is a few homey Horse Badorties touches. In fact, man, since the landlord has evicted me out of my Number One Pad, I will now move into this Number Two Pad. This is my lucky day, man, a brand-new pad. A new pad and a second-hand school bus, which reminds me, man, I must get out of my new pad AT ONCE and go to New Jersey, man.

9 About a Spoonful

Now, man, that I am outside my two-pads in the fresh air and on the way to New Jersey, let me sit down on this Tompkins Square Park bench and eat my newly-purchased container of yogurt. Take into my person tiny Transylvanian bacteria which will digest the valuable precious contents of my stomach for me. Where, man, is the spoon I should have put in my satchel?

No spoon, man. I must find one, that is definite. However, I do not wish to travel back to my Horse Badorties two-pads as I will only get locked in a repetitive cycle and be there all day. I must find a spoon out here, in the world. Shouldering my umbrella, man, I walk on, knowing that a spoon will turn up.

What is that music I hear, man, floating out over Fifth Street? That is fantastic saxophone playing, man. Somewhere in one of these buildings, man, I must find the source of that music and sign the saxophone player into the Love Chorus.

Where exactly is it coming from, man. Seems to be emanating from this brick building here which is falling down. Filthy half-starved wild dog in the doorway, growling over a chicken bone.

"Stand aside, man."

Definitely, man, the saxophone music is coming from up there, up these stairs. The music of a finished artist, man, like myself. Finished and done for. I wonder what music school he was thrown out of. I am getting closer to the sound, man, climbing up the stairs. How beautiful the way that saxophone drowns out the music of all the Puerto Rican radio stations playing in this building.

It seems to be coming from this floor. Yes, man, it is coming from that door at the end of the hallway. A very advanced sound, man, the river-flowing ego-gone supreme-school sound and I am beating on the door the orchestral tom-tom. Saxophone playing stops.

Door opening, spaced-out suspicious paranoid saxophone player staring at me, man, with his ax in his hand.

"Was that saxophone playing coming from here, man?"

"No, man, it wasn't."

"It was great playing, man."

"All right, man, that's different."

"Exactly, man, and now that we understand each other, just tell me one thing, man, one especially important fact about your musical development, man, and that is, man, do you have somewhere in your pad, man, a spoon so I can eat this motherfucking container of Bulgarian yogurt."

"Yeah, man, I guess I do, come on in."

10 The Wonderful Yellow School Bus

"Man, that yogurt has given me new strength and vitality, man, I'm ready to leap over a tall building in a single bound, help me to the door, man, I have terrible indigestion, man, from those motherfucking Transylvanian bacteria, man."

"Why don't you smoke a little of this, man?"

"You're right, man. Let's be civilized."

The sax player takes out a stash of Peruvian mango

skins, the mild vegetable stimulant to help you see the iguanas in your eyeballs.

"Allow me to ignite it with my Japanese match, man."

Scratch . . . scratch

"Here, man, try a wooden match."

"Right, man . . . man. . . ." Smoking Peruvian mango, man, a green high, speaking of which, man, I have to get on the highway to New Jersey and buy my school bus.

"Dig, man, I've got to split, man. I'll see you tonight at St. Nancy's Church on the Bowery."

"OK, man, I'll try to make it."

A rare find, man, a trained musician to add depth to the Love Chorus in its last week of rehearsal. My lucky day, man, and now, man, NOW? Yes, man, now, with my mind liberated by Peruvian mango skins I race down the stairs and in super-fast lightning flash astral-hero compressed time sequence, I arrive at the Port Authority Building, buy ticket, and stumble onto the bus just as it leaves the station.

I am riding on a bus to New Jersey, man, watch the scenery flop past, guy at a gas station, gone past, kid on a front lawn, gone past, Two Guys From Brooklyn pants factory, gone past, great Jersey swamp spreading out and out.

"Finkfield."

Finkfield, man, that's my stop.

"Hold everything, man, my umbrella is stuck in the seat, man, don't close that door, here I come, man. . . ."

Charging down the aisle, leaping down the steps, hitting the ground, man, the Knight of the Hot Dog is on his spiritual quest!

The junkyard, man, stands right alongside the highway, beautifying the state with ten thousand old vehicles piled up, and I am entering it slowly, man, humbled in the presence of all this junk. It exceeds my wildest dreams, man, and I am turning down the lane here into an incredible MOUNTAIN OF JUNK! My dream, man . . . this is last night's dream, man, coming true to show me I am on the right path buying a school bus. Look, man, look at the incredibly numerous broken piles of old batteries wheels parts iron heaps altars of stashed crap, man. And ahead of me, standing in the middle of it all, is the owner, man, Mr. Thorne. I'd recognize him anywhere, man, because of the spaced-out look in his eyes. A collector, man, of weird objects—a burly guy standing there, man, looking it all over, in an old busted hat and falling-apart trousers. He's the Pope of Junk, man, look at him, looking around with deep religious feelings moving in his heart, man. I have found my guru.

"How's it going, man?"

"Afternoon."

"I called about a school bus."

"Here she is over here, near-perfect condition, just needs a little work on the steering box, the ball-joints, and the brake shoes. She squeaks a little when you brake her."

"Minor details, man. I can see that it is a road-worthy bus. I have an instinct about such things."

"Is that so? Well, over here now, is somethin else you might be interested in. It's an old air-raid siren. . . ."

"Man, I am looking for an air-raid siren for years, man!"

"Got an old minesweeper here alongside it."

"Right, man, throw it in the bus, I'll use it to look for lost wristwatches in my pad . . . help me lift it in, man."

We're loading the bus, man, with valuable precious objects. I feel like I've come to heaven, man. What is that I see lying there on the ground, all rusted-up with handles and bands, a piece of modern sculpture which I can sell to the Whitney Musuem. "What's this here, man?"

"This is the braking mechanism from an old subway car, an antique you might say."

"Give me a hand with it, man, load it in."

Man, this school bus is tremendous, man. I can get so many fantastic objects in it, go anywhere, a floating junk-pile, man. "What's this thing lying here on the ground, man, all these poles and pulleys and springs, man?"

"That's a fabulous piece of machinery, son, belonged to a feller known as the Great Springboard. Just a local boy, got into the big time, toured all over the world. Used to shot hisself a hunnert feet in the air on this thing and come down in a net."

"What happened to the cat, man?"

"Out at the World's Fair over in New York a few years

ago, he sprung up in the air and came down on his head in the parking lot. After the funeral, his mother came out here and sold it to me."

"How much do you want for it, man?"

"I don't figure on sellin it just yet. I kinda like to come out here now and then and look at it and think about that boy, springin off through the air."

"I know how you feel, man. It is obviously a valuable precious content of your junkyard. Well, how much do I owe you for the rest of the stuff, man?"

"Three hunnert bucks takes it away."

"Right, man, here's a check from the Fourth Street Music Academy . . . hey, is this your dog, man?"

"I wouldn't pet that dog if I were you, son. He smells pretty bad, you'll have to throw your clothes away if he rubs up against you."

"Here, man, come here and give Horse your paw."

His paw, man, is encrusted with grime and oil and his coat is covered with burrs and grease and he is the perfect watchdog for my pad, man. "How much you want for this dog, man?"

"Ten bucks takes him away."

"All right, man, here's a check for three-hundred-ten bucks, man, and now I've got to split in my school bus."

"Here's the owner's card, son. Be careful backin out."

The dog is in the bus, man, and I am behind the wheel, and starting up the motor.

"Come back again, son. I got a lot more stuff here you

should look at. Got an old airplane engine here, if you like to fly."

"I'll be back tomorrow for it, man. Don't sell the airplane engine to anyone else. I can use it to fan my studio."

The old school bus is moving, man, listen to that engine purring. It handles like a tank, man, I can hardly steer it, what an advantage. Turning it around, man, in the junkyard, practically tears my arms out of the sockets. I should have remembered to get a driver's license, man, but there is plenty of time for such things later because now, man, NOW, I am off and away, onto the highway and heading back toward New York City, with a school bus at last, man, piled with precious objects and a dog.

Fenders rattling, windshield broken, hole in the floorboards, wind rushing up through—my cool school bus, man. Maestro Badorties is wheeling along at last, man, forty miles an hour in his own valuable vehicle. The things I can do with this bus, man, the incredible adventures and fifteen-year-old chicks I can get in here, man. But the first thing I must do is slow down, man, there is a sharp curve up ahead. . . .

. . . slowing down, brakes working all right, but the wheels, man, do not seem to be turning in the direction I must go in. There is a little dirt road, man, head for it directly, go down here bumping off the highway and down this narrow steep dirt road, fighting with the steering wheel which turns, man, but nothing happens and I cannot stay on the little dirt road either, man, I am careening along with the brake pedal all the way to the floor and it is not working, man, there are no brakes, I'd better shift it down, man, double clutch down into low gear, there is no more low, man, the clutch is gone watch out, man, the bus is going off the dirt road and over this bank, man, and down, man, my life is rushing past me, man, there is Van Cortlandt Park before my eyes, man, and I am bouncing down this bank of rocks and dirt and going down into New Jersey swamp grass, man, down into a foot of water and mud and coming to a stop, man, in a swamp of tall weeds, with my wonderful school bus, and my dog is looking at me.

"That's it, man. We've had it."

We are mired in fetid grassland with pussy willows coming up past the windows. I'd better get out before the fucking thing sinks completely under, man, and the state police come and discover I have no license to drive my school bus. How awful, man, to leave behind my school bus with air-raid siren, minesweeper, and subway-braking mechanism, man.

Can't get the fucking door open, man, so it is out the window with my satchel and umbrella, man, and dropping down into the swamp. Now to get my dog out. "Come on, man, crawl out of there." Water, man, and muck, and there, man, coming over the hill is a police car. No time to get my dog out, man. The police will have to remove him. I've got to get the hell out of here, man, through these tall pussy willows, man, and continue off through the swampland, which feels exactly like the floor of my apartment, man, about a foot of water and mud. I can go through it easily, man, with trained footsteps, they'll never catch old Horse.

Keeping my umbrella low, man, I proceed through the swamp grass and there are the state troopers, man, swarming over the school bus and scratching their heads, man, looking at my dog behind the steering wheel.

I am out one school bus, man, but it will be returned to the owner of the junkyard, along with the rubber check I gave him, and now, man, I am slipping far away from the scene of my wonderful yellow school bus. Through this grove of trees, man, I can watch as they bring down a tow truck, man, and haul out the old bus. It's sad in a way, man. But I realize now, man, that instead I should buy a used mail truck.

11 The Mad Dialer

Back in New York City again, man, coming up out of the subway into the Lower East Side with swamp mud in my shoes and pussy willows up my pants leg. It is night-time in the city, man. Another typical Horse Badorties day has gone by, man. I had to walk ten miles through a swamp, I missed my Love Chorus rehearsal, and I have got to make a hundred phone calls immediately. Here is my favorite phone booth, man, on First Avenue, and here is my special mercurized dime, man, which allows me to call again and again, without paying anything.

"Hello, man . . . there's a shipment of organic carrots on the way, man, are you interested in a few bunches. . . ."

"Hello, man, will you get out your *I Ching*, man, and look up this hexagram I just threw, number fifty-one, nine in the fourth place, what is it . . . *shock is mired?* Right, man, I'm hip, I lost my school bus in a swamp. . . ."

"Hello, baby, this is Horse Badorties . . . sing this note for me will you, baby, I need to have my tympanic cavity blown out: *Boooooooooooooooooooop*!"

The night is going by, man, passing on starless and deep, with millions of people going around here and there, and the Fearless Phoner is calling every one of them.

"Hello, Mother, this is Horse. Did I, by any chance, on my last visit leave a small container of Vitamin C tablets, little white tablets in an unmarked bottle . . . yes, I did? Good, I'll be up to get them soon, man, but don't under any conditions take one of them."

"Hello, man . . . is this Dial-A-Chicken? . . . tell me something, man, do you deliver to phone booths. . . ."

"Hello, man, Horse Badorties here . . . listen, man, I'm sorry I didn't get over to your pad with the Swiss chard, man, but I was unavoidably derailed for three days, man. I was walking along, man, and I saw these kids, man, in the street, playing with a *dead rat*, man. I had to go back to my pad to get a shovel and bury it, man. You understand, man, kids must not be imprinted with such things. Look, man, I'll be over soon, I'll be there at . . . hold on a second, man, just a second. . . ."

Coming directly down First Avenue toward this telephone booth, man, is Sundog the fiddler. I don't want to see the cat, man. It's not that I don't dig him, man, but I cannot stand the sight or sound of a violin, man, it makes the most horrible noises on the face of the earth, man, combining a cat's gut and a horse's tail to produce fiendish screeching, so I must therefore utilize the famous Aleister Crowley black magician make-myself-invisible-to-all-others-technique, man, whereby I can walk right through an Arabian marketplace, man, and not be seen by a single person. It is all in the willpower, man, and I am now crunching myself up in the phone booth and at the same time forming a psychic screen around myself so that as Sundog the fiddler walks by, man, I will be rendered completely invisible to his gaze.

"Hey, Horse, man, what are you doing curled up in the phone booth, man?"

"I'm making a thousand phone calls, man, and am passing out in the process."

"You're in luck, man, I happen to have a bit of brandy in my fiddle case."

"DON'T OPEN THAT FIDDLE CASE, MAN, UNTIL I HAVE CLOSED MY EYES! Alright, man, go ahead, my eyes are shut."

"Here you go, Horse, in this flask."

"Thanks, man. I need something to set my cells on fire

and numb my brain . . . good stuff, man, lot of bite in it, where did you get it?"

"I know this old guy, man, lives out in the New Jersey woods, man. He makes the stuff himself. Puts all kinds of things into it, man. Puts a piece of rat's tail in it, man, just the very tip of a female rat's tail."

"Man, you're kidding me."

"I wouldn't kid you, Horse. I've watched him make it. I've got to split, man, you want another snort before I go?"

"No, man, one is enough to kill me, man, thanks." Closing the phone booth door, man. How terrible, man. I have been poisoned by a fladdler, man. It's the kind of thing you come to expect from cats who play the fucking fladdle, man. The sound of the fladdle warps their minds, man. And right now, man, essence of rat's tail is coursing through my bloodstream and making its way to my brain, man. I can feel it locking in there, man, and forcing me to make hideous rat-faces at passers-by, man, contorting my nose lips cheeks eyeballs, as I phone onward, man, into the night.

"Hello, man . . . dig, man, I'm talking in code, do you want any carrots . . . right, man, carrots, I wouldn't put you on . . . give you orange visions, man. . . ."

The reason I love this particular phone, man, is because when you close the door, a little fan goes on inside the booth. How wonderful, man. I am feeling very weird nonetheless, man, from all this phoning which is affecting my eustachian tubes producing a state of imbalance, man;

the booth seems to be floating through space, off through the night, man, as the Mad Dialer dials, setting up a carrot deal so incredibly detailed and carefully mapped, that nobody, not even me, man, can follow its path. . . .

"Hello, man . . . this is Horse Badorties, I've got a deal cooking, man . . . stop shouting, man, I can't hear you . . . right, man, now I remember—I already have your bread, that is, man, I had your bread until today, man, when a strange thing happened, man, which you will find hard to believe . . . don't go away, man, I'll call you back in five minutes."

Here comes Jimmy Dancer down the street, man, he's just the cat I want to see. Plays the four-string banjo, man, and he is always interested in some health-food carrots, free from poisonous spray. "Hey, Dancer, man, how are you doing?"

"Horse, man, I was just going over to your pad to see you, man."

"Terrific, man, I'm working a deal. . . ."

"I'm going to Canada, Horse. I need my overcoat back, man. It's cold up north."

"Your overcoat, man?"

"Yeah, man, you remember, I loaned it to you last fall when you went away to teach music at the little girl's camp in the mountains. Remember, man, a big black fucking overcoat?"

"Don't ask about that overcoat, man. Ask me about anything else in the world, man, but don't ask about that overcoat."

"What's wrong, man. What happened to the overcoat?"

"It's too terrible, man. I can't tell you."

"What do you mean, man?"

"I can't tell you, man. Just take my word for it. Your overcoat died an honorable death, man, but I can't go into the details, they are too hideous."

"The overcoat's gone, man?"

"I know how you feel about your overcoat, man. I feel the same way, and that is why I am sparing you the details, man, of what happened to it."

"Hey, man, this is too much."

"Yes, man, it is too much for the mind to bear and therefore I am screening you from a fact you would only have to repress later on. In the meantime, man, here is a little pouch of Panama Red turnip greens, man, which will ease your pain."

"Thanks, man, but I sure wish I had that overcoat. A cat laid it on me years ago, man, when we were traveling down Route 22."

"Right, man, and now it's gone to overcoat heaven. Listen, man, if you practice deep breathing, man, you won't need an overcoat, you'll be able to melt snow with your asshole. Look at me, man, I'm not wearing an overcoat and it's the middle of summer. Say, man, before you go to Canada, come and sing with the Love Chorus. We're doing a show in a few more days, man, and I need some baritone voices, man, St. Nancy's Church on the Bowery, eight o'clock tomorrow night."

"I don't know, man."

"Don't take the loss of your overcoat so hard, man. Today, man, I lost a school bus, a dog, an air-raid siren, a minesweeper, and a subway-braking mechanism. St. Nancy's, man, tomorrow night."

"All right, man, I'll try and fall by."

"Do that, man, and now if you'll excuse me, I have to make fifty more phone calls. . . .

". . . hello? . . . hello, man, Horse Badorties here, man. Man, I'm sorry I didn't get over to you with the tomato surprise, man, but dig, a very strange thing happened, man. I was walking in Van Cortlandt Park, man, and suddenly I saw this airplane overhead, man, running out of gas. The cat was circling low, man, looking for a place to land. I had to guide him in, man, for a forced landing, man, and it took quite a long time, which is why I'll be late getting to your pad, man. . . ."

". . . hello, man, listen, man, I've been having fantastically precognitive dreams lately, man, I am digging the future every night, and last night I had a definite signal, man, that the flying saucers are about to land. That's right, man, I wouldn't kid you, and dig, man, I am getting everyone I know to come up to the roof of my pad, man, to watch the saucers land, as there is a possibility I'll be carried away, man, into the sky and taken to another planet. . . ."

12 Commodore Schmuck on the Water

It is morning, man, the sun is coming up along First Avenue into the phone booth. I have done it, man. I have spent another entire night in a phone booth, making calls as numerous as the sands of the Ganges. I seem to remember setting up a perfect carrot deal, man, if only I can figure it out. And now, man, to get out of this phone booth, into the Bardo of Rebirth, man. The door is stuck, man. I am trapped in my booth.

Here comes a lone figure down the street, man, coming out of the gray light of morning. It is the saxophone player, man, carrying his ax, on the way home from a gig. I am banging on the door, man, and here he comes, man, to the rescue, kicking open the booth.

"How's it going, Horse?"

"Help me, man, I've been all night in this phone booth, man, I need oxygen and a hot dog for breakfast. I've seen the truth, man. I've got to buy an armored United States Treasury Department truck. Let's go, man, up the street, and get a cup of coffee."

"I've got to get some zzzzzz's, Horse. I'll catch you later."

"Right, man, take it easy. I'll see you at rehearsal tonight."

I have got to get some zzzzz's myself, man. But not back at my pad, man. That four flights of stairs, man, would kill me. And besides, man, I have to visit NBC today and alert them about the Love Concert. So I will go to Central Park, man, and sleep in the grass and then, later on, walk over to NBC. A perfect plan, man.

But first, man, I must go immediately to Barney's Men's Shop, man, and buy myself a new suit for my visit to NBC. It is essential, man, when dealing with high-level executives to look the part.

"TAXI!"

Zoooooooom

Barney's Men's Shop, man, here I am, looking through the suits. I'd better find one that's marked down, man, as I used my last rubber check on that motherfucking school bus. Here is a beautiful suit, man, for $185. It's my size, too, man. The only thing that is necessary now, man, is to remove from my satchel my special four-pointed, four-color ball-point pen and select the ink which matches this price tag. Then, man, by simply moving the decimal point over one place, and adding a zero to the end of the figure, I have found a suit that is marked down to

$18.50

"Yes sir, may I help you?"

"I'll take this suit, man."

"Yes sir, cash or charge?"

"Cash, man, I only came in for a pair of sock, but I couldn't resist the cut of this suit. It will fit perfectly, man, and I am going to wear it out of the store."

"Very good, sir."

In the dressing room, man, changing out of my old in-shreds Horse Badorties suit and climbing into my in-perfect-condition-marked-down-for-special-sale Barney's suit. It looks terrific, man. Just what I need for NBC.

"Yes sir, that will be eighteen dollars and fifty cents, plus tax. Shall I dispose of your old . . . ah . . . suit?"

"If you would, man, please. On second thought, man, you'd better not, you'd better put it in an airtight bag, man, and let me take it away for burial." I cannot let this suit fall into hostile hands, man. It is precious, like my valuable toenails which must be sacrificially burned, man, after cutting. Black magic, man, is everywhere. Terrible things might happen to me if this suit fell into the wrong hands. Puerto Rican witch doctors, man, performing weird rites, man, with chickens and my old suit. I can't have it, man, I already have stabbing pains in my beak, man, just thinking of it.

"Here you are, sir, and thank you for shopping Barney's."

"Right, man, stay cool." And out I go, man, into the bright sunlight, man, which is too bright, man, I must put on my special shades, man, completely black except for fifty pin holes in each lens. Makes you feel like you are walking around in a wire cage, man, with the optical field split up into a pin-hole pattern, so you can hardly see where you're walking, so therefore, man, I'd better take a cab.

"TAXI!"

Cab pull directly over to curbstone screech. Bearded cabby wearing shades.

"Wait'll I get my umbrella in, man, can you shove it up there in the front seat, thanks man. Central Park, man, anywhere at all."

Zoooom cab moving out, weaving through traffic stop-lights clang-bang through the gears. Cab-man karate. Feint little tap with the bumper going uptown into the sunlight. Driver looking over his shoulder, cutting smoothly nearly killing man with an armload of packages, knifing along, turning the wheel, moving ahead.

"All you need in this cab, man, is a fan, man, to cool yourself."

"I'm cool, man."

"Right, man, and you can be even cooler with this handy-dandy fan, man, nothing like it for soothing vibes." There is of course one other cooling procedure suitable to this moment and that is to remove from my vest-pocket this large gold-plated ball-point pen, a souvenir of the Empire State Building. The pen, man, is hollow inside, and by opening it and shaking it I dispense into my hand one wrinkled neatly-folded-at-each-end health-food smoke, man, of salty seaweed harvested by Portuguese fisher-women and dried on stones.

Light up, man, draw deep, give smoking stone seaweed to cabby.

"Thanks, man."

Fearless cabby, man, go anywhere, smoke anything.

Horse Badorties and spaced-out cabby smoking sea-weed, smiles of sunlight wreathing thc air. Riding along in the flashing light.

Cabby suddenly stoned in middle of Lexington Avenue so what man go anywhere any conditions. Fly automatic pilot, know city insidc-out, stoned, drunk, flaked-out, you-name-it I'll get you there. Perfect coordination, weav-ing the traffic, floating the traffic, everybody fuck-all dreaming.

Come up to hotels fountains bubbling in sunlight, turn-ing onto Central Park South there are the trees, man, we are at the park.

"Right here is good, man."

Zoom over to curbstone.

Pay cabby, give him as tip the rest of the seaweed, man, for use in the rush hour. Give him a rush to beat all other rushes, man.

"Right, man, thanks."

"Hey, man, do me a favor and hang this public announcement in the back of your cab, man. Look, I'll stick it right here. Tell the world about the Love Concert, man, two-three days from now."

And I am stepping out of the cab with umbrella and satchel, man, high uptown. Cab driver take off zzoooooooommmm.

Oh no, man, I have left my precious valuable used rotten old suit in that taxicab, man. I must give chase, man, at once, and retrieve it. On second thought, man, fuck it. That's how it goes, man, life brings mistakes with it too and my suit is now on the way into the hands of the witch doctors. By tonight I'll have terminal pains in my elbow and a rash on my balls, man, with weird dreams about turning into a chicken, man. Chicken-man Badorties, man, it's too horrible to contemplate, it makes my tongue wobble, man, to think of it. So while I am still in good health, man, except for my usual brain tumor, let me turn here, into Central Park, man, into wonderful beautiful Central Park with trees and grass and birds and squirrels. What, man, am I doing here. I should be in Buffalo buying a post office.

Walking along, man, in Central Park, over the grass,

dead tired, carrying my tremendously heavy satchel and umbrella. Why, man, did I get born? To do precious valuable Love Music, man, you remember.

Life, man, is so difficult when you are carrying a satchel that stretches your arm out to the ground. I see a chick ahead, man, pushing a baby carriage. Somebody just got born, man, and is getting wheeled around in the sunshine.

"Here, baby, here is a piece of sheet music for you and one for your baby, bring you good luck."

Chick smiling, baby gooing, that is the life, man, someone to change your diaper and wheel you around. But just wait a while, man, wait about two or three years when they start teaching you how to play the violin. Then, man, you will know pain, in the neck muscles specifically with complications down to the base of the spine, possibly including the feet.

I am going along through Central Park, man, with no phone, no trash pad, no cockroaches, and I feel disoriented, man. I'd better lean against this litter basket, man, and get an energy transfer. Lonely life, man, on the planet Earth. I'd recognize it anywhere, gravity holding me down. Long time ago, man, I used to float around in the sky with a sitar, a celestial musician, man, who has fallen from the heights. The only way to get off the earth, man, is die, and I am definitely dying, man. The all-important question is: Will I be able to take fan satchel and umbrella with me when I go?

Up ahead, man, I can see a fountain, ringed with

chicks, man, hot pants short blue jeans long hair beads, and I am going down the great stoned steps toward the fountain, to where all the chisk are gathered, ass tits pussy for the Love Chorus.

"Dig this music, baby. Tonight at St. Nancy's on the Bowery. When you come just once, baby, then after that I pick you up in the Academy Mail Truck. Just give me your name and phone number, would you, thank you."

Pushing laughter chicks in the fountain, jeans wet water clinging ass chisk everywhere sunshine summer earth and I am circling the fountain, man, with my satchel, laying sheet music on the chicks. "National television, baby, and everyone gets a fan. After singing we retire to the Academy for a midnight snatch. Everyone is bringing food, bring some food along, yes, your telephone number, thanks you, so much."

Stone angels dancing on the upraised bowl of the fountain, dripping with water. Beneath the stone angels is a stoned chick, laughing, long black hair, her dress soaking wet her tits belly ass showing. O Horse Badorties, this too is why you come to Earth, for EARTH CHICKS!

Carrying satchel carrying umbrella, leaving fountain behind. I must not linger at this fountain or I will eat a hot dog from that little shack nearby, there, with mustard and sauerkraut. A Central Park hot dog, man, is instant ptomaine. However, to protect against putrification causing ptomaine, the hot dogs are wrapped in a plastic jacket. How wonderful, man, a plastic hot dog, I'd better have two of them, AT ONCE.

"Gimme a . . . gimme. . . ." What is this I see, man. It is a plastic toy wind-wheel, man, of blue and white on a little stick, man. AN AUTOMATIC PERPETUAL FAN, MAN! ". . . one of these fans, man, make it two of them, man, thanks." And now, man, as I walk along, with this wind-wheel attached into the back of my suit-jacket collar, the motion of my body actually produces a windstream against the delicate blades of the wind-wheels, man, and they are turning. Batteries not necessary, man, and if I run along the blades go faster and the pitch changes . . . running, man, jogging with satchel umbrella and wind-wheel, man. Jogging, healthful invigorating jogging . . . slow down, man, stop jogging or you will collapse with a blood clot in the big toe, man.

I've covered a lot of ground, man, and through the trees is the roof of the Central Park boathouse, man. I HAVE IT, MAN! I WILL TAKE A LONG SLEEP IN A ROWBOAT, MAN, OUT ON THE LAKE WITH NO ONE TO BOTHER ME!

What an idea, man. I am going straight along to the boathouse, man, going to the ticket window, saying to the lady, "Give me a ticket, pleebe." Make monkey-face, stick ears out, roll eyes up, hang tongue down. Ticket lady is sitting in ticket booth, half-asleep, man, and she wakes up suddenly into a Horse Badorties face and jumps, man, with a ticket. And as she hands it through the window, man, I slowly sink down beneath the window, and with only my hand showing I take the ticket and crawl away to the entrance to the ramp that leads to the boats, where I immediately straighten up into nautical carriage, man, for there, ahead, tending to the rowboats is one of the most important figures in the Puerto Rican Navy, Admiral Rodriguez, man, in his official white yachting cap from John's Bargain Store.

Commodore Schmuck salutes the Admiral, who returns the salute, and shows me to my boat, man.

"Hang onto my umbrella a second, Admiral, while I crawl in, as I don't want to drop anything in the water. Giant eels, man, live down there. OK, man, hand it over, thanks."

"Hokay, *amigo,* here you go," says Admiral Rodriguez, giving the boat a little shove, man, and I am going out into the channel, manning the oars, man, making gentle ripples in the water and pulling away from land.

Waves sparkle oars rise, fall, and as the boathouse slips away behind me, man, the roof gleaming in the sunlight, it seems to become a Chinese pagoda. Long ago, man, I was a Chinese boatman, skilled with oars, able to make a boat move fast. The old Chinese boatman vibes are taking over now, man, making the oars really work, moving the boat faster, churning up the water, splash spalash . . . OH NO!

"Stop the boat, man, hold everything. I have to return to the land and call a doctor. I just got a drop of this motherfucking stagnant poisoned water on my lip, man . . . arrrrrggggghhhhhhhhhhhhh!"

Wiping mouth and tongue off on jacket sleeve like wild animal, man, biting at the wool, attempting to remove from my lips before it is ingested the drop of deadly Central Park lake water, man, which is more toxic than the venom of a black mamba, give me galloping typhoid, man. Spitting in the lake "Hock—tooooeeeeee, man!" Open satchel, dig down into dark depths find antiseptic solution, gargle immediately, full-strength.

But what is worse, man, far worse than the terrible cramps and sudden mind lesions produced by this water, is the speaker of a transitor radio in the distance, through which Puerto Rican music is being broadcast, man. Dig down into satchel for Commodore Schmuck naval action earflap cap. Puerto Rican water music, man, cripple, drive insane. Everything is OK now, man. I am in the soundproof hat, and can resume gentle rowing up the channel. I'm getting tired, man, and my feet are getting cold, the poison must be spreading through my body. I had better administer the antidote. Out of my satchel, man, comes Doctor Badorties' huge Ann Page Blue Cheese Dressing bottle, which is filled with clear spring water. Fitted into the neck of the bottle is a number four black rubber two-holed chemistry stopper. A chemist's thistle tube, conveniently shaped like the bowl of a pipe, is passed through the number one hole of the number four stopper. Through the number two hole is fitted a mouthpiece hose. And out of the special Culpeeper's herbalist pouch, I am taking a few sprigs of wild asparagus leaves, and sprinkling them in the thistle tube.

And now, man, I am once again coming up with the award-winning superb-design perpetual Japanese Match.

This small container, no bigger than a postage stamp, upon which the Ace of Spades is embossed, contains actual lighter fluid. By simply unscrewing this little knob I remove the match itself, and strike it against the abrasive surface of the Ace of Spades, producing healthful nonsulphurous fire to light the homemade Horse Badorties hookah.

Scratch . . . scratch

Total failure of ignition. Astronaut Badorties waits in painful anticipation while the ground crew scrambles around inside the satchel. Lift-off is then provided by old-fashioned polluting sulphurous matches which work instantly and lift Astronaut Badorties into outer spaced-out places, man. Floating, man, on Central Park lake.

Now, man, in my sound-proof hat and relaxed brain, I am slipping down under the seat, man, and stretching out on the deck of the boat, man, and going to sleep.

The oars are in, man, and the boat is gently rocking, drifting along wherever it cares to go, man. The gods will navigate it for me, man, and protect the innocent sleeper. To the tides of the holy stagnant pool, man, I commit myself. I am so tired, man, from losing my school bus and running through swamps and phoning all night and rowing out to the middle of this artificial motherfucking poisoned lake. Now, man, in total silence and peace, looking up to the bright soot-gray sky above, man, I am soaking up vital prana; the astral fluid of life, man, swims into my valuable precious falling-apart person.

There seems to be a slight leak in this boat, man. It

was dry when I entered it, but I feel water swirling around my Chinese-Japanese shoes. A minor acupuncture, man, of the Puerto Rican flagship. I cannot investigate it now. Commodore Schmuck is sinking into sleep, man, in order to gain strength for unknown battles to come.

13
Commodore Schmuck Is Betrayed at the Bay of Crabs

"Hey, Raoul, dere ees a boat floatin' all eetself on de water."

"Come on, *muchachos,* les' get dat boat an' go for a ride!"

"Eeet's too far out. How we gon' get eet?"

"I'll sweem out for eet."

"Hokay, *hombre, muy bien.*"

Jump een de lake, sweem out for de boat. We de Hundred an' First Street Knights, *hombre,* we sweem good, get a holt ob de rope hangin' down from de fron' ob de boat an' bring her bock to shore.

"Hokay, here eet ees."

"Come on, *muchachos!*"

"Hey . . . wait a secon', somebody ees een dees boat. Look, he layin' een de bottom ob de boat."

"Eet's hokay, he ees a heepie, he don' mind eef we use hees boat."

Climbin' een, we all climbin' een de heepie's boat. "Don' wake heem up, *muchachos,* he look bery tired. Don' step on heem. Come on, *muchachos,* all aboar'."

"Dees boat hob a leek een eet."

"Das' alrigh' . . . we can . . . take the oar, José. . . ."

"We got too many een dees boat, mon."

"Row hard, *amigos,* row!"

"Hey, Raul, I tellin' you, look at de boat, our boat she is takin' a lot ob water. . . ."

"Row, *amigos,* row!"

"Fuck eet, mon, the fron' ob dees boat ees goin' under."

"She's goeeng down. . . ."

"Jump, *muchachos,* she ees seekeeng!"

I'm having some kind of dream, man, that somebody is trying to push me down into the toilet bowl again, man, somebody trying to drown me. Fuck this dream, man, I'd better wake up. It must be time to leave my pad . . . man, WHAT'S GOING ON! Where am I, what, man, what?

Green scummy water, man, all over me, and kids,

man, all around . . . I'm in some kind of green dish, man . . . what is it, man, a Puerto Rican bathtub? There are trees, man, you're in Central Park, man, and your boat is sinking. Quick, man, grab your satchel, there it goes.

Like lightning, man, Commodore Schmuck grabs the Bardo of Death by the handle. Hang onto that satchel, man. Watch it, man, the umbrella is floating away. I've got it, man, I have saved it from instant disintegration in this water. The boat, man, is completely under, and I am standing in it, man, in three feet of poisoned water, man. I've always wondered how deep this fucking lake is.

And now I've got to walk across the bottom of it, man, to shore. Step out of the sunken boat, man. Commodore Schmuck's flagship has been sunk from under him. Walking, man, I am walking once again through muck and slime, man, across the bottom of the Central Park lake, man, which is filled with bottles and tin cans and creeping death weeds, man. How hideous, my afternoon nap has been ruined, man, in a most fiendish way. This lake water, man, will finish me. This much of it, man, would kill anything. Once, man, I saw a crab crawl out of this pond, and he was covered, man, with oily slime. Crawling along dazed, as I am now. This crab, man, was walking along, and he was TRYING TO CLIMB A TREE. Trying to get away from this motherfucking polluted water, man, which I have just been completely submerged in, man, swallowing countless mouthfuls. You should have seen the crab, man, trying to make it up the roots of the tree. Grab hold with his claw and lift himself up. I watched him all day, man. By sundown, he was halfway up the tree.

And I am halfway to shore, man, dripping wet, and I have apparently lost my hearing, man. The immersion in the horrible waters of this lake, man, has rendered me totally deaf. The effect has been immediate, man, the water must have gotten down into my eardrums. Perhaps I can shake some of it . . . Man? I AM WEARING MY COMMODORE SCHMUCK HAT! I'M NOT DEAF?

No, man, you can hear. You will not have to produce your symphonies in total silence, man. Thank goodness, man, that even though all other parts of my body, from asshole to elbow, were completely soaked with water, my alimentary ear canals remained sealed. In a few hours, man, there will be nothing left of me but two ears walking across Central Park.

14 The Fan Man in the House of the Dead

I am standing on the shore, dripping wet, man. I must therefore crawl up through these bushes, man, and disrobe. Off with my brand-new suit, man, which I am wringing out and hanging on a tree limb, man, in the sun.

Here comes a cop, man, and he sees my suit hanging out to dry, and he is coming over to the bushes in which I am hiding my naked person.

"What's going on here?"

"Look, man, I fell in the fucking lake with my new suit on, man, and I'm trying to dry it out."

"You fell in the lake? How did that happen?"

"I slipped, man. I was standing on a rock looking at a fucking fish and I went down."

He feels my clothes, man, just to make sure. "Yeah, they're wet all right, aren't they?"

"It's a drip-dry suit, man, it'll be dry in no time."

"Well, keep out of sight."

"Right, man, I'm hiding in these bushes, man, thanks."

Cop, man, walking off, twirling his billy stick. Fortunately, man, he did not want to look inside my soaking-wet satchel, man, wherein are traveling various organic health-food materials which do not bear the Good Housekeeping Seal of Approval.

My suit is hardly dry, man, but I cannot hang around in these bushes all day, man. I've got to put it on again, slightly damp. That's how it goes, man. It's what I get for coming to Central Park, man, instead of going to Van Cortlandt Park.

All right, man, I am once again walking along in my soaking suit with my squeaking water-shoes, dragging my way across the park, toward NBC. There is a bird, man, hopping along, talking to himself. I will freak him out, man, make birdsong.

"Criiiiiiicccccccckkkkkkk, criiiiicccck, tweeeeeeee," says the bird, and Horse Badorties says

"Criiiicccccccckkkkkkk, criiiiicccck, tweeeeeeee."

Bird turn around, look around, spooked, wondering—where is that sound coming from, man. Is there some other bird around?

It is only me, Horse Badorties, running through his bird-lifetimes. I must, man, get everyone in the Love Chorus to make flapping motions with their arms. To resurrect the bird memory. That is definite.

Someday, man, I will get myself together, flap my arms, and split the cosmos. Go into nirvana, man, get me some rest on the big white couch of bliss. Not today though, man, today I must go to NBC.

But first, man, I must sit down on this isolated park bench, man, flung up here in the bushes by some thoughtful juvenile delinquent. And even though my brief case is filled with water, fortunately, man, my herbal leaves and twigs are all contained in handy plastic bags recommended by Good Housekeeping, man, and hermetically sealed against the onslaughts of the Puerto Rican frogmen who tried to drown me. I have dry smoke, man, and now that I am in this quiet little spot, let me roll a tremendous joint of banana flakes in licorice paper, and though it is as big as a gorilla's finger, smoke it all completely entirely down to the last stub-end, which I shall swallow. And then, fortified by the life-giving brain-fog of banana smoke, I rise.

But before I rise, man, why not roll still another one, to make sure I'm really stoned, because sometimes, man, in my condition, it is hard to tell.

Sprinkle flakes into paper, make cylinders of fingers, roll perfect joint, and light.

I am still sitting, man, not walking. Walk, Horse Badorties, walk in your wet suit. OK, man, I'm going, I'm moving, the big bird is floating down the day. I seem to be coming out of the park, man, as well as out of my mind. What, man, does that sign say . . .

76th Street

Jesus, man, what am I doing up here, NBC is down in Rockefeller Center. But there ahead of me, man, is the Museum of Natural History. Let's go look at the stuffed animals.

Go up the steps of the museum and enter the dark building into dark hallway, where a herd of old gray elephants are walking along tall, man, with glass eyeballs.

Look, man, they have a stuffed gorilla family here, standing in a fantastically vivid life-life arrangement of foliage and rocks to simulate an African mountain range. The grass slopes down, and beyond it, curving in incredibly real fashion is a painting of great and further distances, the African plains. A gorilla is standing in his garden of Eden, man, looking down the hillside. Couple little baby gorillas sitting around fucking with some berries and the old lady gorilla is sitting in the doorway with her saggy gorilla tits. And coming up the hill through the far-away jungle trees of this marvelously accurate and beautifully arranged diorama of jungle life is a natural biologist scientist collector, man, with his net, and he is coming to stuff the apes and take them back to his weird house.

Faint smell of decay in the air. Hides must give off a little stink every day. But dig, man, the sound of the great ventilators, making a tremendous hum in the background. Man, I must find the source of that sound. Here's the office of the curator, man, go directly in. Secretary sitting at a desk, looks up. "Yes, may I help you?"

"Fan Man. Here to repair the fan. Some trouble with the ventilator, we received a call at the main office."

"Oh, let me see . . . that would be maintenance. I'll ring them . . . *hello . . . this is the curator's office. There's a fan repairman up here . . . yes, there's some trouble with the ventilator. . . .*"

"The pitch is slightly off, baby. We can always tell this sort of thing by the sound it makes."

"*Very good, thank you* . . . a guard will be here in a few minutes, sir, to take you."

"Thanks you so much."

"I've noticed it has been a bit stuffy in here today."

"Yes, the pitch is probably slightly off in the main blade." Dig into satchel, bring out tuning fork, strike on kneecap, hold it up to secretary's ear, give her A440 vibrations per second in her ear canal. "There, baby, that's the proper pitch."

"How interesting. You tune it like . . . a musical instrument?"

"Exactly, there is an amazing correspondence between

fans and musical instruments, excluding, of course, the violin."

"Here is the guard."

"You called, Miss Winston?"

"Yes, would you take this gentleman to the . . . where exactly do you have to do your work, sir?"

"At the main unit . . . the big fan, man, it must be in the basement somewhere."

"Right, I know where you mean. Just follow me, sir."

Repairman Badorties and the guard walk down the hall, man, and down some steps, and down another hall, and open a door marked

Staff Only

and go down some more steps, man, into the sub-basement of the lonely house of death, man, into the cold stone cellar, man, where the hum is growing louder, man. The great roaring drone of the supreme fan is exciting my eardrums to the visionary state, man. Man, what a sound, open the mind completely out, tremendous vibrating drone:

"BRAAAAAAAAAAAAAAAAAAAAAUUUUUUUUU UUUUUUMMMMMMMMMMMMMNNNNNNN."

And there it is ahead of us, man. Enormous, the great Museum Fan, man, with numerous ducts connecting it to the entire building. This is the Chief, man, speaking his great word to the dead:

"BRAAAAAAAAAAAAAAAAAAAAAUUUUUUUUU UUUUUUMMMMMMMMMMMMNNNNNNN."

And now, man, I will answer, putting in a Horse Badorties Dalai Lama bass note:

"BRAAAAAAAAAAAAAAAAAAAAAUUUUUUUUU UUUUUUMMMMMMMMMMMMNNNNNNN."

The guard, man, is scratching his head. "How's she doin?"

"The pitch seems all right, man. I can't understand the problem."

"Seems all right, does it?"

"Operating perfectly, man. But I'll just check it out on the oscillator." Removing from my satchel, man, the Doctor Badorties army surplus stethoscope, man. Putting the rubber-tipped prongs in my ears, man, and applying the sensitive listening disc to the heart of the Great Fan. Oh, man, this is fantastic, man. This is the primal voice, man, singing into my stethoscope. I hear a thousand songs in there, man, and a couple of dinosaurs running around talking to each other with bass notes beyond belief, man. They have some dinosaur bones on the fourth floor of this pad, man, and I'm picking up their vibes. And I see by the label this fan was built by the Passaic Fan Company. Looks like I'm going to have to make another trip to New Jersey, man, and purchase one of these fans on long-term credit with a rubber check down.

"The pressure of the sound waves is all right, man. Everything is checking out. The only thing I can suggest, man, is that perhaps some kid threw a hot dog down one of the ducts."

"You think so?"

"It's happened before, man. I'll have to go back to the main office and get my duct-diving suit, man. Without it, the pressure would be too great. You see the suit I'm now wearing? I wrecked it only an hour ago, climbing through the fan duct at the Pan Am Building."

"It's dangerous, is it?"

"Right, man, I'll be back in an hour or so. You might want to take this piece of chalk from my satchel, man, and go through the building, marking each of the vents with an *X*, so that when I get back, we can go straight to work."

"Will do."

And up we go, and up again, and out the side door of the museum goes fan-repairman Badorties.

15
The Fan Man Gets the Shaft

And now, man, I must proceed directly to NBC. Here comes a bus, man, must run. "HOLD THAT BUS, MAN!"

Difficulty getting enormous umbrella in the door, it is caught in the driver's wheel.

"Watch that umbrella, will ya mac."

"I'm sorry, man . . . sorry. . . ." In the confusion, drop a few pennies into the coin box and continue on the way, riding for four cents downtown, bus moving jerking forward and I am careening backward to the back of the bus and accidentally strike strap-hanging man behind the knees with my satchel and he falls straight to the floor.

"Sorry, man . . . terribly sorry . . . coming through. . . ."

It's hot on this bus, man. Time for further fanning. What is this, man, it is not working. The Central Park lake water has disintegrated the points of my fan. And it has also shrunk my suit, man, I can feel it getting tighter every minute. And there is Rockefeller Center, man, stop the bus.

Dingle . . . ding . . . dingle.

"Excuse me . . . coming through. . . ."

Bus jerks to a stop, satchel swings forward, strikes same man behind the knees and down he goes again, man, to the floor of the bus. "Sorry, man . . . excuse me. . . ."

Leaping off the bus, man, and crossing the street, into the incredibly large lobby of Rockefeller Center, footsteps echoing, echoing. To the Information Booth, man.

"Yes, sir, may I help you?"

"Ace Messenger Service. I have a large umbrella for *The Tonight Show*. My instructions are to deliver it directly to the Director of Programming. It's for the show tonight."

"Programming . . . that would be Mr. Reynolds, fourth floor."

And so forward goes Horse Badorties, man, to the executive elevator. Press number four button and up we go, man, up, up, up.

Elevator opens onto long silent hallway. Here is a

Men's Room, man, I'd better just step inside and see that my appearance is suitable for this high-level conference, for which I had better brush my tufts of hair.

Through the door, through another door, and into the shining spotless tiled head, man, and there is a mirror and there I am, man, oh no, man.

Hair flying out, beard filled with twigs and stagnant lake weeds, my tie is on sideways and coming out of the sleeve of my jacket which has shrunk up to my elbows. The cuffs of my pants are up to my knees, man, and the entire ensemble is covered with Central Park muck and grime. The effect, man, is one of nightmare proportions. How can I discuss business in this condition? I look like I just fell down the elevator shaft. There is only one solution, man.

Back into the hallway and walk along, man. Arrow on the wall and a sign saying

Programming

Therefore, man, before I turn this corner, I must drop to my hands and knees, that's it, man, and now I crawl along this corridor, toward the desk of that secretary up ahead. She sees me, man, she is getting up, looking astonished, and I am crawling forward, man, dragging my umbrella and satchel.

Crawling along, man, toward her desk. She comes toward me, her face filled with concern. "Are you all right?"

". . . fell . . . down . . . elevator shaft. . . ."

"Oh my God!"

"Floor . . . above . . . door opened . . . accidentally . . . stepped through . . . I have an appointment. . . . Mr. Reynolds . . . could you. . . ."

"I'll call the doctor . . . an ambulance. . . ."

"Yes, please . . . I may be . . . seriously . . . herniated big toe . . . but first, please . . . I have to see Mr. Reynolds . . . utmost urgency . . . my appointment. . . ."

"What is your name, sir?"

"Badorties . . . Maestro Badorties, Resident Director of the Fourth Street Music Academy . . . fell twenty-five, maybe fifty feet, landed in puddle of water which had collected on top of the elevator . . . narrow escape. . . ."

"Mr. Reynolds . . . there is a Mr. Badorties out here . . . he fell down the elevator shaft . . . he has an appointment."

The immediate sound of scurrying feet, man, and the Director of Programming bursts out of his office, man, toward my prostrate form.

"What happened . . . good god, Miss Hodgekiss, the man is badly hurt . . . call the doctor . . . and then call the superintendent. That damned elevator has been on the blink for a week. Yesterday a delivery man was trapped in there."

"Yes sir."

"Mr. Reynolds . . . in my satchel. . . ."

"Yes, what is it?"

Director of Programming bending over, filled with concern, man, helping me open my soaking wet satchel, from which I am able to draw a single dry piece of music.

"This is the music, Mr. Reynolds . . . which we will be singing on the show."

"Show?"

"Didn't my secretary . . . my appointment was for this afternoon. . . ."

"I don't recall. . . ."

"On the Lower East Side, Mr. Reynolds, in the slums, run-away teen-age chicks are singing church music . . . the concert is just two days away . . . I seem to have dislocated my head . . . Love Concert in Tompkins Square Park. . . ."

"Run-away teenagers?"

"Fifteen-year-old chicks . . . fracture of the kneecap, see it protruding . . . singing church music, man . . . one million sheets of the music you have in your hand have been distributed all over the city, we expect a considerable crowd. . . ."

"Concert?"

"The day and hour is written on that sheet . . . possible laceration of the greater fibula. . . ."

"I think we'd better get you to the hospital, Mister . . ."

"Badorties, Maestro Badorties of the Fourth Street Music Academy . . . contusions of the . . . young girls who have run away from home come to live and sing at the Academy, which welcomes them with broken arms. If you could help me to my feet. . . ."

"Yes, of course . . . can you walk. . . ?"

"I will use my umbrella as a cane . . . a most important

concert . . . I assure you it has news value . . . can you help me to the elevator . . . I will go directly to my family doctor . . . over at Bellevue. . . ."

16
Far Out, Man

On the street once again, man, with satchel and umbrella, and I have gone to NBC, man. I have informed the network of the Love Concert. Now it is up to the gods, man, to make it happen. Look, man, it is quitting time, and all the secretaries and executives are on the street, man, hustling along. Everybody flooding into the subway, man, and Vice-president Badorties must descend into the darkness with the rest of the working class.

Going through the turnstile, standing on the platform, and here comes the impossibly-crowded car into which not a single more person can fit, they are already hanging out the windows. It stops and a hundred more people get on and I am one of them, man, and my umbrella is another one, and we are inside, standing straight up, crushed together in the car.

It is the middle of summer and we are packed stuffed wedged in the subway, and there is absolutely no air, man, to breathe. And I cannot get to my fan, man, my arms are pinned.

Riding, riding, five hundred people in this car, man, all of them pissed-off, hate the boss, going nuts, dropping dead, fainting outright but supported by the crowd.

Mumble mumble kill somebody fiendish energies collect down in this tunnel thrown off by countless workers every day. Kill the boss death push in front of subway car fart sweat foul. Can't stand this subway, man, it overloads the brain, man, but I cannot get out, even when the doors open, I am jammed too much in the center and my umbrella is stuck up in a strap handle. Reading the subway ads, people getting off, getting less crowded, reading the subway ads, shrink your hemorrhoid, easy terms borrow needlessly when you must, our family makes this sauce for generations out of stenographers, you've come a long way, baby. A LONG WAY! Jesus Christ, man, where am I, I must be at the Lower East Side by now, man. It does not . . . look familiar, man, as I step out of the subway car.

Up the subway steps, man, walk up, see where I am.

I am on Brooklyn Heights, man, there is the sea below. A wild wind is blowing and the sun is dropping toward the ocean. The water is gold and the tugboat goes through the gold.

I am with you again on the Heights, man.

17 The Elephant Dance

I am sitting on a park bench, man, on the cliff-heights of Brooklyn, looking out across the water. How peaceful, man, I've got to get out of here, Brooklyn is the end of nowhere. Alright, man, I'm off the bench and walking. Lead weights in my brain, man. It is nearly impossible, man, to function with shrinking Japanese-Chinese shoes and my head on backwards. Carrying satchel and umbrella, flopping along the street. Horse Badorties coming apart, going along. When I was a little kid, man, I used to dig a hole in Van Cortlandt Park everyday and crawl into it.

What is this I see, man, it is a toy store. Must go in, man, and look around. I'm in the store, man, a little old Brooklyn toy store, and I am buying not one, but two music boxes, man.

"Thank you, sir, and your change."

Out of the store, man, before I buy more. What a wonderful purchase. Little music box, you are my little orchestra of steel men, man. Play same notes over and over, perfect coordination. Let me now wind up the box with this Japanese key—seems to be stuck, man. The motherfucker is stuck already. I am not five yards away from the store and the music box is jammed. I cannot take it back, man, that would not be playing the game. This is my music box, man. It's a good thing I have another one.

This other one is working, man, the two little figures on top of the box are dancing around, round and round and the little steel musicians are playing, plinka-plinka. This toy, man, will afford me hours of musical pleasure.

Booooooiiiiinnnnnnnnnggggggggg!

What is that sound, boooooiiiiiinnnnnnnngggg, man, like a broken spring. It is a broken spring, man. What a tremendous deal I just made, man. Two Japanese music boxes that don't work. Four figures waiting for the music. A perfect moment, man. Everlasting No-Play. *Waiting for the dance*. It's nirvana music, man. Complete silence.

Here is the subway entrance again, man. So much of

my life, man, is spent under ground. "One token, pleak." Give token-lady freak-face, see her eyes pop, and I am going through the turnstile and here comes the train and I am on it and going all the way back to the Lower East Side.

Here I am, man, getting out of the subway on the Lower East Side, man, climbing the steps, hitting the street once again, man, at Cooper Union and St. Mark's Place, back to my people, man. Feel the filth and dust, man, blowing into my eyes and the stench of piss and shit and vomit and old beer cans, man, up my nose. We're back, man, where we belong.

St. Mark's Place, man, with one headshop after another, man, where I will SELL A FEW FANS! Go into this weird psychedelic emporium, man, with rotating lights give me a headache and incense make my eyes water, how wonderful, man. Over to the counter, man, where the manager is sitting in a high silk hat.

"Listen, man, what you need to stimulate sales is one of these fans, man, dig."

Hauling out fan, clicking the switch, nothing happens. "The batteries are dead at the moment, man, and it is filled with water, but anyway, man, you get the idea—for heads to cool themselves."

"How much you want for the thing?"

"I buy them for one dollar and ninety-five cents and I sell them for one dollar and ninety-five cents. People ask me why. I'll tell you why, man—they are holy objects, which make music, a little humming note, and that is why I cannot allow myself any profit on them."

"I'll give you a buck and a half."

"Terrific, man, that's even better for my soul, I'll be losing money on the deal."

"How many you got with you?"

"Just this one, man, and I'd leave it with you, but it's my only sample. However, I have a tremendous shipment coming in any moment, man."

"I'll take a dozen."

"Groovy, man. How much do you want for this special battery-powered back-scratcher in the showcase, man."

"Cost you one dollar and ninety-five cents."

"A necessary item, man, haul it out."

And now I have made another purchase and filled my already incredibly heavy satchel with yet another precious valuable object, a battery-powered back-scratcher with a long handle, man, and a little plastic hand on the end of it, which vibrates back and forth. Apply to third eye, stimulate visions. I will sell it as a chakra-massager, man, and that way it will be a holy object for which I will not be able to charge more than one dollar and ninety-five cents. Another Horse Badorties scheme, man, by which I can't make any money. Get out of this store, man, before you turn into a saint.

Across Second Avenue, man, and down the street to First Avenue, and further down—to Tompkins Square Park, man. And dig, man, there is the saxophone player blowing some notes on a park bench with a trombonist, man, and the trombone sounds like an elephant coming through the jungle, man, and the saxophone sounds like some weird prehistoric bird. Man, these are musicians.

I must get this on tape, man, it is essential, sound like animals gathering around a waterhole, wild, wonderful, quite a crowd gathering around, man, and I am setting up my two tape recorders, and now, man, I am also taking out of my satchel my incredibly weird instrument, man, my moon-lute. It's got a round thin sounding box on it, man, and four strings that go up a bridge shaped like the neck of a snake with a dragon's head on top of it. The strings are tightened by four huge wooden knobs, man, which look like ears. It is the weirdest fucking instrument I have ever seen, man, and when you play it it sounds like you are choking a hundred Chinamen. The incredible moon-lute is tuned, man, with the saxophone and trombone. Saxophone smile, man, and the trombone slides open his eyes and smiles too, man, and now, man, we will play some music.

Moon-lute rhythms, man, to drive you crazy. Intricate plinka-plinka, man, all those Chinese cats, man, in the moon-lute strings, dancing and jumping around screaming, man, plinky-plink.

It is an incredibly weird sound, man, the likes of which no one in Tompkins Square Park has ever heard. It is so weird, man, it is driving me crazy to play it, but at the same time it is so perfectly beautiful, man, because I am master of every opening and closing rhythm pattern known to the mind of man, and in moments like these, man, when I am playing them all, I know, man, that music should be the only thing I ever do. Which is why I am going to become a used-car salesman instead, man. What a wonderful sound, man, the Horse Badorties omniscient musical genius moon-lute sound, I should be hiring a mechanic at this very moment, man, to fix my mail trucks when I buy them.

Fingers going, man, fifty fingers, all over the strings, progressions, outward, upward, backward, downward, resolution of chords in unthought-of never-before-discovered hierarchies of Horse Badorties specialized musical perfections, man, how I wish I was eating a clam sandwich instead of fucking around with this blissful ecstasy, man.

This is so beautiful, man, I have to split over to my pads immediately, someone might be trying to phone me about some carrots. Loveliness abounding, man, in superb musicianship of moon-lute, saxophone, and trombone, crowd standing awestruck, man. Man, these cats know how to play.

Yes, man, Horse Badorties knows how to play, been playing since two years old, and now we are playing back two thousand years, man, back through the centuries, man, in musical excursion back through the ages, different lifetimes coinciding—I knew you there, man, when we played lyre and were thrown out of the gates of Athens, and further back, man, I used to bang an Egyptian piano while you played the dog-headed flute and you played the Etruscan bagpipe, man, and we ran through the woods with the Babylonian police after us.

This is simply marvelous music, man, I'm so happy, I'd better stop now, man, I have to go and buy a submarine. Oh, man, how this little moon-lute performs, in petite figurations, first position second position barre chords of unearthly beauty learned in a Pompeian jail. And the trombone and saxophone are gut musicians, man, go anywhere, play anything, not afraid to leap around with their axes, man, they don't give a damn, they've been shuffling around spaced-out for ages, man, the trombone sounds like an old hippopotamus, man, saying good morning—HOPPOPITAMUS? Man, that was my dream last night, man, I was playing music with an elephant and a hoppopitamus, man, and here we are, man, saxophone and trombone and moon-lute, man, making jungle sounds in the park, fingering and sliding, microtone picking of supreme swiftness, saxophone making jungle rivers of smooth notes and a hollow wooden boat going along on that river, what music, man, vision music ineffable. Horse Badorties, man, though he is fucked-up, knocked-down, turned-around, blown-apart, worked-over, pasted-together, and falling apart, can play. In spite of all luckless stars, man, we are making great music. This is when I feel really free, man, but I don't deserve it, I should be making a telephone call to my dentist.

Here we go, man, working toward the release, man, the crescendo climbing climax, here are a quick few sixty chord changes and some impossibly intricate fingernail-destroying hammering-on techniques and backwater jive and a symphonic swelling out and a Chinese ogdoad and a cartload of beautiful melodies all at once and then, man, as we conclude on exactly the same plane, man, in pure and doubt-free rhythm perfectly together, the crowd shits itself, man, hollering and clapping, and chicking hanging around, flashing eyes.

Saxophone player says, "All right, man."

Trombone says, "Cool, man."

Horse Badorties says, "Yes, man, but it will sound even better when we add the sound of a tremendously large museum fan which I am purchasing in Jersey tomorrow."

"Do you have a group, man?" asks the trombone.

"Man, I've got groups all over the country, but especially I have got a group rehearsing tonight at St. Nancy's Church around the corner, man, and you come there at eight o'clock we will smoke oatmeal in the choir loft and sing some fantastically beautiful wonderments, man."

"Sounds like a gas, man."

"It's done with fans, man. Dig, I have to split now, to take care of the numerous events of my life, man."

"All right, man," says the saxophone. "We'll be in touch, man."

"Right, man, and here is how. Within my satchel is a pair of walkie-talkies, man, and you take one and I'll take one, man, and we will remain in constant contact, MAN!"

Saxophone takes walkie-talkies and I walk away and over to the edge of the park and give it a test, man. "Hello, man, can you hear me, man?"

"Yeah, man, you are comin' in clear."

"Alright, man, cool. I'm leaving the park, man . . . and crossing the streeep . . . crackle . . . sputter. . . ."

I must get a dozen more walkie-talkies, man, and have musicians situated all over the city, playing simultaneously. I can hear the saxophone, man. He's blowing some notes into the walkie-talkie.

"Sounds beautiful, man, I can hear it perfectly. We've done it, man, at last."

Crackle . . . sputter . . . crackle. . . .

Fading out, man, it's starting to fade, but it will come back when the time is right.

"Hey, man, who was that cat playing the weird instrument?"

"Cat named Horse Badorties, man, he came over to my pad one day to borrow a spoon to eat some yogurt."

"He knows how to play the fucking thing, man, whatever it is."

"Yes, man, that is true. Wait a second, man, I hear something on his walkie-talkie. . . ."

"Hello . . . hello . . . crackle . . . sputter. . . . this is Horse Badordies . . . crackle . . . man . . . crackle. . . ."

"OK, man, you're comin in clear. . . ."

". . . crackle . . . sputter . . . right, man . . . I hear you too . . . something about a mongolian idiot . . . see you . . . crackle . . . later . . . sputter . . . man. . . ."

18
Horse Badorties' Four Pads

Walking along Avenue A, man, with satchel umbrella and here is a little girl playing in the street, man, with her one-armed dolly. The kid needs something, man, to protect her from the music her uncle makes on the gourds. "Here, *muchacha,* have a music box."

"*Muchas gracias,*" she says, taking the music box, touching the little lace dress of the lady dancer on top of it, man. It's too bad it doesn't work, man. She's giving the figures a little push.

"... plinka ... plink ... plinka. ..."

It's working, man, the music box is going, there go the dancing figures, man, around and around. And there goes a fantastically sexy blonde chick, man, up Avenue A QUICK, MAN! After her, going after her, man. The chick is on the road, man, she's a run-away teen-age blonde chick, man, with a knapsack on her back and soon she will have Horse Badorties on her, too, through the power of my personal magnetism, charm, and the promise of a free pad.

"Here you go, baby, here's a piece of sheet music for the highway. You want a place to spend the night? It's getting late, you want a safe place to stay."

"All right," she says, looking through me quickly, and seeing the purity of my intentions to screw her.

"It's just around the corner, right along here, step over the garbage cans. Just a second, baby, I'll buy a couple of long juicy Puerto Rican submarine sandwiches, such as you have never tasted, filled with sausage, onions, peppers." Into the store, man.

"May I halp you?"

"Gimme a can of begetable soup, man, make it two cans."

"Fiftee cen', *por favor.*"

"Thanks, man, this is your lucky day. Tomorrow I'll be bringing in a tremendous museum fan with twenty-five ducts on it and we'll direct one through your ceiling into this store."

"Ducks?"

"Right, man, flying south to San Juan. See you later, man. OK, baby, I've got dinner, we just have to go up these stairs here . . . watch out for the first step, it isn't there . . . up we go up. . . ."

Up the four flights of stairs behind the blonde chick, a beautiful chick, man, with a wonderful sweet ass in traveling blue jeans, in old sneakers, ankles, and army jacket, a liberated fifteen-year-old chick, man, who will go anywhere, including bed with Horse Badorties. What is this? There is my landlord on the fourth floor, placing a huge bolt and several boards across my door.

"What's going on here, man, that's my pad you're boarding up."

"YOU SONNA MA BITCH, I KILL YOU!"

"Relax, man, what's the trouble?"

"You not pay the rent for six months, you ruin the apartment, you son bitch!"

He's red in the face, man, and green in the fingers. Wants some bread, man. "All right, man, don't blow out your capillaries, I'll write you a check at once, man, right now."

"DON'T GIVE ME NO SONNABITCHIN CHECK, YOU BUM!"

"Don't wave that hammer in my face, man, you might hit yourself in the head with it. Look, man, I assure you, this check is perfectly good, I just received some money for an article on an abominable footprint from *Argosy* magazine."

"You get the hell out of my building, dat's all, Mister, just go."

A voice calling from the landing below, a lady calling the landlord: "Hello, Mr. Patrutchka, is that you up there?"

"Yeh, it's me, what's de matter?"

"My ceiling is caving in with water you better come down here."

Landlord turning to me before he goes down the steps: "You be out of here in five minutes, take your stuff and go!"

"All right, man, if you'll be good enough to remove the boards from the door of my pad. . . ."

"You wrecked the apartment, you sonbitch bastar', I never get it clean again."

"A small matter, man, a single girl scout could clean it up in an hour. Give me the hammer, man, I'll open the door and take my things out immediately, man. You go ahead, man, and attend to the ceiling below."

"In five minutes, you be out, unnerstand, or I call de cops."

"I understand completely, man, stand aside, baby, while I. . . ."

Hit the door, man, and knock the partition right out of it. There goes the landlord, man, down the stairs, going out of sight, gone. "All right, baby, come this way, down the hall, quietly."

And we go down the hall, the chick and I, to Luke the Buddhist's old pad, which the landlord does not know I have the key to, and open the door and go inside. "Here it is, baby, my number two pad."

The door swings open, man, to the Buddhist monk's previous pad, man, which he kept perfectly neat and tidy. I have made only a few small additions of Horse Badorties homey touches.

"Sure is a lot of junk in here."

"Art materials, baby, serving as camouflage for a secret passageway, which you will see momentarily. Follow me through that pile of trash cans and old rags, step over that mound of dirt and broken dishes crawling with roaches and come over here and help me move this tremendous wardrobe chest stuffed with bottles and rags. That's it, shove it out from the wall, and what, baby, do you see before you?"

"A hole in the wall."

"That is correct, baby, a hole in the wall, which I took the precaution of chopping out yesterday. If the landlord should by any chance discover that I am living in this number two pad, it won't matter, because we will now slip through this secret passage—go ahead, baby, through those broken slats and falling plaster—through this hole in the wall to my Horse Badorties number three pad."

"Gee, there's a lot of junk in here too."

"Yes, baby, and it was not easy to get these piles of sheet music and garbage bags through that little hole in the wall. Now help me swing the wardrobe back in place to cover the hole, baby, that's it, and now we are entirely safe from the landlord, here in the number three pad, just keep your voice low."

"Doesn't anybody else live here?"

"I have the whole floor now, baby."

And now, man, we can eat our begetable soup, if we can locate the stove. Feeling around through old cardboard boxes and empty cans, here it is, man. Kick, send flying different piles of crap, getting precious valuable objects out of the way, man, and lighting the stove. "And now, baby, out of my satchel comes a handy can opener, and we can cook the soup right in the cans as there are no pots available that are not already filled with scientific mold experiments. We just sit the cans directly on the flames."

"The labels are on fire."

"Yes, baby, it cooks quicker that way. We'll be eating in no time, canned soup, of no possible value to the human system. Have a seat, baby, anywhere at all. The altitude is completely informal, take off your knapsack and relax, Horse Badorties will watch over it for you, baby. Where are you coming from, baby?"

"I was in Provincetown."

"Do they have any mail trucks for sale there, do you know?"

The soup, man, is bubbling up, it is hot.

"I have some spoons in my knapsack."

"Great, baby, this is the life, with soup and spoons and

I think I hear the landlord outside in the hall, going nuts."

Creep quietly over to the door and listen to the sounds in the hallway:

". . . sonamabitch . . . no come back . . . kill de sonnabitch. . . ."

And away he goes, man, down the steps, thinking I am gone, man. We are safe. Life is good.

"And now, baby, let us partake of an after-soup smoke, inhaled directly through this specially imported Hindustani coconut-bowl dope-hookah. Of course I never use it for such criminal activity. Instead, I am loading it with tiny nutritious flour-based alphabet noodles, made of ground-up artichokes and spinach . . . drag deep, baby, let's get healthy."

Chick and Horse Badorties smoking alphabets and passing into the alpha-waves, and I see stretching before me my entire life from when I was a little Horse Badorties in Van Cortlandt Park, which reminds me, man, I must go there tomorrow. After I sue the landlord, man. I must call my lawyer this evening, man. A simple suit based on a stuffed-up toilet in the hallway, down which some thoughtless tenant flushed a Turkish bath-mat. Landlord has refused to repair; privation of tenant, violation of sanitation code, A through B.

"This is good smoke, man."

"Yes, it is manufactured by three little old Italian ladies, based on a time-honored recipe. Let us fill the bowl again and enjoy their family secret."

And now for a little music from the moon-lute, man, sweet gentle Horse Badorties love songs, man, to put the chick in the mood.

"You play nice."

What a sweet blonde chick, what beautiful blue eyes, what nice skin, what gorgeous boobs, what wonderful luck we have found each other and I am playing to her, I'd better knock off playing these captivating love songs, man, and begin chopping another hole in the wall, from this pad into number four pad.

"Baby, I am going to insure us against further intrusion, by lifting this ax and driving it . . ."

Crash

". . . into the wall. . . ."

Sending plaster and wall slats and nails and cockroaches flying through the air. It is hard work, man, that is enough for today. "Soon, baby, we will be able to move through the wall to my number four pad."

"Out of sight, man."

"Yes, but not entirely, baby, for through this brand-new crack I've just made in the wall, we can now see next door, to a PERFECTLY CLEAN PAD, how wonderful, we will soon be there."

19
Hawkman Lives!

"Yes, baby, we are going to be all right, everything is cool and speaking of cool, let us go up to the roof, directly above, and cop a view of the city. Come on, baby, it's an unforgettable scene, I can't remember what it looks like I haven't been up there in so long, LET'S GO!"

And we go out through the hole-in-the-wall, moving the wardrobe, and fight our way across number two pad and out the door. Down the hallway is a staircase to the roof, and we climb the steps and kick open the roof door, and step out, onto the rooftop.

"Dig, baby, the skyline, with swooping seagulls, and over there is the East River, maybe I'll buy a canoe. And over here, baby, is a piece of artwork, produced by a local primitive. Dig the huge drawing of the big yellow bird." We cross the roof, and view the painting, of a great-winged bird traced on the rooftop and beneath it, written in huge yellow letters, the name

HAWKMAN

"Roof art, baby, worth a fortune. Hawkman, the Puerto Rican kid who wanted to fly." I'm far-out, man, looking out over the rooftops, like Hawkman himself, and I am flying, man, to the big clock in the distant tower which says EIGHT O'CLOCK?

"I've go to get to rehearsal, baby, I've got to. . . ."

Just stand here, man, and let your vision sweep far up to the great Manhattan buildings, rising up in the dust and soot. Horse Badorties, man, having a taste of good old samadhi, feeling like the Dalai Lama. Once knew a woman who thought samadhi was a town in Ohio. Samadhi, Ohio man, oneness with the contemplated object, whose energies stream forth as subject and object become one in rapture as, in this case, man, I have become one with the clock tower. EIGHT O'CLOCK, man, I've got to get the fuck out of this rapturous blissful state of oneness and get my ass in seventh gear, over to the church without further blissfulness of spirit.

"OK, baby, I am splitting. Take care of my pads for me and help yourself to any valuable precious objects you find. I'll see you later."

It would be better and faster all around, man, if I went down by this fire escape, thus avoiding the landlord. Here I go down the creaking dangerous falling-apart fire escape, past my number two pad, man, where I must first open the window and stop in and get my umbrella and satchel. Where are they, man, buried somewhere, must change my shoes, read a book, eat something, get out of here, man, do not get hung-up. Alright, man, I'm trying to. Who is that at the door? It is the chick, man, coming back in.

"Right, baby, I'm just leaving, there is my satchel on top of tin-can mountain, watch out, baby, tin cans are falling down all around into new artistic patterns, and here is my umbrella in the bathtub, and I am taking off out the window and down the fire escape . . . so long. . . ."

Going, I am going, creak creak . . . down . . . down . . down . . .

There goes the weird guy. Here he is back again, sticking his head in the window.

"Leave this window open, baby, to air the place out. So long . . . so long . . . man. . . ."

Creak . . . creak

There he goes again, down the fire escape. Weirdest guy I ever saw, looks like he just crawled out of a fishbowl. Well, I'll stay with him tonight and go to San Francisco tomorrow.

On a nearby rooftop, watcheeng, ees Hawkman heemself, watcheeng all de booldeengs, who come, who go, what cheek ees seeteeng alone een a pad weeth de weendow open. Hawkman moob from hees towereeng perch. Over hees shoulders ees worn an old sheet, hees cloak. He leap from one rooftop to another, and go quietly ober de edge ob de roof an down de fire escape an look en de open weendow, where de cheek ees seeteeng.

"Cha cha cha, baby."

"Beat it, man."

"I'm comin' een, baby," say Hawkman, an he flap on tru' de weendow, an land on de floor, an de cheek, she run for de door, but Hawkman, he a fast hombre, he queeker dan Speedy Gonzales, he got de cheek, an he plank her down.

"Lemme alone, man," says de cheek.

"Take off you clothes, baby," say Hawkman, "so you don' get hurt."

Walking along the street, man, carrying my satchel, what is that music, man, coming out of my satchel. Opening my satchel, man, I perceive that saxophone music is coming out of my WALKIE-TALKIE! The saxophone player, man, is contacting me.

"*. . . crackle . . . sputter . . . honk . . . crackle. . . .*"

"Hello man, hello this is Horse Badorties, man. I read you. Where are you, man? You sound tremendously far away, man."

"*. . . crackle . . . honk . . . crackle. . . .*"

"Right, man, I read you. Horse Badorties here, man, where are you?"

"I'm standin in the doorway right alongside you, man."

"Hey, man, there you are! Terrific, man, these walkie-talkies are tremendously powerful, man, wouldn't you say?"

"Definitely, man."

"Dig, man, come to the Love Chorus rehearsal with me."

"Alright, man, but first let's smoke a little of this," says the saxophone.

And he removes from his case a tremendous cigar-shaped joint, composed of several papers rolled together and no doubt filled with a mild stimulant, perhaps ground-up sesame seeds and rice flour.

"Allow me, man, to apply the award-winning Japanese match, man. . . ."

Scratch . . . scratch. . . .

"Here, man, try my Zippo."

"Right, man, the good old USA. Terrific, man."

Smoking down tremendous joint.

"It's sprinkled and flavored throughout, man," says the saxophone, "with various chemicals."

"Absolutely, man, to preserve and promote shelf-life."

Fantastic dynamite angel-smoke, man, my head is going through the side of the building. Man, I am an old bunch of bricks. I am STONED, man, I am floating through different places up and down the street.

"Let's play some music, man," says the saxophone.

"Definitely, man. I have to be at my rehearsal half an hour ago."

We tune up, man, and we play, playing swift sweet melody.

"Is good for you, baby," say Hawkman, on top ob de blonde cheek.

"Oh, you lousy spic bastard," say de cheek, struggleeng a leetle.

"Walk along while we play, man, through the street, man, and over to the church. My eyes, man, are hurting me, wait a second, man, while I get my opalescent bird-wing sunglasses out of my satchel. I'm stoned out of my mind, man. Where are we, man, in the A & P?"

"You're on the street, man," says the saxophone. "Dig the traffic."

"Crazy, man, I can hear gongs in there somewhere."

"Look, man," says the saxophone, "I don't want to

bring you down, man, but you are standin there with your head turned, man, listenin to the street. It looks weird, man. A cop might wonder what you are listenin to, man."

"Gongs, man. Listen to them."

"You are putting me on, man." Bend over, listenin to the street. "You are right, man. There are gongs in there."

"Yes, and what is more, man, there is Puerto Rican music coming out of that restaurant. Walk faster, man, before it envelops us."

"You should try and dig their music, man."

"Yes, man, I'd like to dig it, six feet under the ground, man, in a hole, and bury it. Here's St. Nancy's, man, let's go in and bolt the door behind us."

"How you like eet, baby?" ask Hawkman, smileeng as he go out de weendow.

"You stink, man."

"Take it easy, *muchacha,*" say Hawkman, flyin eento de air.

20
The Doctor-Foot-Itch Miracle Cure

"Alright, Love Chorus, it is time for some advanced musical technique which will lift us up to the final plateau before our performance. Observe the incredibly weird face I am about to make, rolling my eyeballs up into my head so that only the whites of my eyes are showing. And now I am contorting my lips so that my teeth appear to be fangs munching. Will all of you please make that face, let's go, roll eyes into head, very good, up, up, and curl lips back . . . now, dig, man, now you have to form your hands into reptilian flipper-claws on little short arms as if they were growing out of your chest. Right, that's it. And what do we have, man, we have tyranosaurus-rex, man, bend the thumbs under, man, this is a creature who lived previous to the opposing thumb, that's it, MAN!"

I think they all have it, man, twenty-five chicks and a couple of cats, man, making prehistoric reptilian Horse Badorties faces, man, with wiggly fingers. "Feel it coming on, feel the ancient long-buried genes rising up. You used to be dinosaurs, man, and now let's walk around being dinosaurs and tyranosaurs and let's SING, man, without the sheet music, sing and make faces, one two three. . . ."

Listen to them, man, they are beautiful. The only way to make trained musicians out of untrained musicians is to get them to forget, man, all their hang-ups about not being able to do music. Then, man, when they are making a face so incredibly weird that they have forgotten about their musical blocks, their soul will sing as it is singing now, man, right on pitch, perfectly. Walking up and down the aisle of the church, man, a parade of reptiles. When you make these faces, man, it is impossible to think, as they are precognitive faces, man. When you do them your brain gets smaller.

"Very good, Reptile Chorus, that is all for tonight. Our performance is now scheduled for seven o'clock Saturday night in Tompkins Square Park. I have reams of publicity out all over time, and here are some printed sheets announcing the special program. Give one to everyone you know."

I've got to get out of here and make it back to my four pads and ball my one chick, man. I've had a long day. Everybody is going down the stairs, saxophone player, trombone player, priest, chicks, the Love Chorus, man, of busted-up strung-out Lower East Side losers, man, and we came by candlelight, man, and we sang.

"That chorus sounds good," says the saxophone player, as we go out the church door.

"Yes, man, but when the fans arrive, then, man, then you will hear something."

"It sounds great now, man."

"I'm gratified to hear that, man, as every musician is filled with uncertainty, and my chief uncertainty, man, is about when my fucking fans will arrive, because without the sound of those fans, man, the pinnacle will not be reached."

"They really make it, do they, Horse?"

"These fans, man, are little gods, man, and they make the sound, man, in which all other sounds are contained—they make the whirring sound of AUUUUUUU UUUUUUUUMMMMMMMMMMMMMMMNNNNNN, man, and I am depending on that sound, man, to make the Love Concert the most incredibly perfect musical event in the history of the earth."

"Where did you learn music, Horse?"

"When I was two years old, man, I was made to study

the violin, man. Did you ever wonder, man, why my head tilts over to one side and my chin touches my shoulder? I'll tell you why, man, it's from cradling that motherfucking violin, man, in my neck and holding it with my chin, man, as a child. It ruined my posture for life. I'll see you tomorrow, man, I've got to get home and ball my new chick, man. I'm foaming at the mouth, man, I haven't been laid in a millennium. So long, man, keep in touch by walkie-talkie."

"Right, man, take it easy."

Horse Badorties I am Horse Badorties hurrying off to see my new blonde chick, wonderful fucky-wucky, hurry, man, along the Avenue and around the corner and down the street. It is dark, man, no landlord around. I can go straight up the front steps without fear, man, with my heavy satchel umbrella and exploding balls, man. Blessed relief is at last in sight.

Up the steps to get on top of her and eject the valuable precious contents of my gonads into her snatchel. Here I am, man, going through the door of my number two pad, and pushing aside the wardrobe and going through the hole in the wall to my number three pad, man, and there is my chick, man, there she is! Opening her lovely red mouth to speak love to me, man.

"A dirty lousy Puerto Rican spic piece of scum crawled in your goddam window tonight and raped me."

"My window?" Panic button *on*. "What did he steal?"

"He raped me, man, that's what he did."

"Listen, baby, this is important. Did he tamper with my tape recorders or other precious objects?"

"You fucking lousy bastard!" Chick is out-of-line, man, throwing an old butter dish at me.

"Stop making a scene, baby. Valuable sheet music may have been stolen." I must make a quick check of everything, man, of every single content of my pad. Look around, check things out, here is the telephone, man, I must make a phone call immediately, my fans have been delayed too long. Dialing, dialing. . . .

"I hate this fucking city," says the chick.

"That's funny, the phone seems to have gone dead. Did he fuck with my telephone, baby? Is that what the motherfucker did? Wait a second, man, now I see what's going on, this is one of my spare telephones, it comes completely loose from piles of different refuse. It has never been connected at all. Thank goodness, baby, communications were almost severed."

"I'll have to get a VD shot."

"Not necessary, baby, I'll tell you why. Has to do with psychic mind-control power. Autosuggestion is enough for the organism. Think to yourself that you've already had the VD shot, and your cells will react accordingly."

"Oh, fuck off, man."

"Listen, baby, I will tell you the true story of Doctor-Foot-Itch. In fact, I will write it up this very moment for *Argosy* magazine. I had this rash, man, between my toes. Musician's feet, they call it, from keeping tempo with the toes inside plastic Japanese shoes. Stung like a sonofabitch, man, between every one of my toes. Agonizing awful constant burning tickling motherfucking itch, drive me crazy. I hurried out to the drugstore, baby, and laid down a buck and a half for a tube of Doctor-Foot-Itch, the miracle itch reliever. I could hardly walk any longer, man, but I crawled directly back to my pad and laid the tube down and quickly misplaced it and lost it completely in my action-painting pad. As a consequence, I never applied Doctor-Foot-Itch to my feet. I never even took it out of the box. BUT MY FEET STOPPED ITCHING THAT VERY NIGHT! And they have not itched me since. Doctor-Foot-Itch is here in the pad, baby, buried somewhere, doing his quiet work. Indeed, it was a miracle itch reliever."

We sit, man, staring at each other. The chick, man, I can read it in her eyes. She doesn't want to fuck Horse Badorties. She's had her fucking for the day. The Puerto Rican paratroopers, man, beat me to my chick. She's putting on her army jacket, man, and picking up her knapsack. "Where are you going, baby?"

"I'm going to the YWCA and take a shower."

"Listen, baby, you can take a bath here. I'll scrub your back. The tub is around here someplace . . . here it is, baby, it's merely filled with a thousand old tin cans, let's clean them out together. Let's turn over a new leaf, start clean, baby, from the beginning. We'll take baths and bake bread and hang some oilcloth on the windows, make the place our own little love nest, man, what do you say?"

"So long, man."

The chick is splitting, man, out through the hole in the wall, man, and gone out of my life, man. Horse Badorties, man, is alone once more.

21
It's Dorky-Day Once Again!

"Dorky dorky . . ."

(It is morning, man, on a new day, and I am stumbling around my pad, repeating over and over again) :

". . . dorky dorky dorky dorky dorky dorky dorky dorky dorky dorky dorky dorky dorky dorky dorky dorky dorky

dorky dorky dorky dorky dorky dorky dorky dorky dorky dorky dorky dorky dorky . . ."

(Constant repetition of the word *dorky* cleans out my consciousness, man, gets rid of all the rubble and cobwebs piled up there. It is absolutely necessary for me to do this once a month and today is dorky-day):

". . . dorky . . ."

(There is a knock at the door, man, go answer it.)

". . . dorky dorky dorky dorky dorky dorky dorky . . ."

(It is the knapsack blonde chick, man, she has come back, she has returned. I wave her in but I cannot stop my dorky now.)

". . . dorky . . ."

"I got a VD shot."

". . . dorky . . ."

"I tried hitch-hiking out through the Lincoln Tunnel and the cops stopped me."

". . . dorky . . ."

"I figured maybe I should stay in the city a while longer. I thought it must be a sign."

". . . dorky . . ."

"What's going on, man, what's all this dorky?"

". . . dorky . . ."

"I brought some breakfast for us . . . some bread and jelly."

". . . dorky dorky dorky dorky dorky dorky dorky dorky dorky dorky dorky dorky dorky dorky dorky dorky dorky

dorky . . ."

"Christ, man, knock it off, will you?"

". . . dorky dorky dorky dorky dorky dorky dorky dorky dorky dorky dorky dorky dorky dorky dorky dorky dorky

dorky . . ."

"You're driving me up the wall, man."

". . . dorky . . ."

(Another knock at the door, man. It always happens on dorky-day. It is the saxophone player, man.)

". . . dorky . . ."

"How's it going, Horse?"

". . . dorky . . ."

"What's up with Horse, baby?"

". . . dorky . . ."

"I don't know. He was like this when I got here."

"... dorky ..."

"Hey, Horse, what's all this dorky, man?"

"... dorky ..."

"I have some bread and jelly in my knapsack. Do you want some?"

"... dorky dorky dorky dorky dorky dorky dorky ..."

"Thanks, baby, don't mind if I do."

"... dorky

dorky . . ."

"What is it, raspberry?"

". . . dorky dorky dorky dorky dorky dorky dorky . . ."

"Strawberry."

". . . dorky . . ."

"Hey, Horse, man, knock it off, man, and we'll play some music."

". . . dorky . . ."

"He won't answer you. I only met him last night, but I know he won't answer you."

". . . dorky dorky dorky dorky dorky dorky dorky dorky dorky dorky dorky dorky dorky dorky dorky dorky dorky

dorky dorky dorky dorky dorky dorky dorky dork dorkyy dorky . . ."

"I think maybe he's composin some kind of song, baby."

". . . dorky . . ."

"I thought I might stay with him for awhile, but I can't stay here, not with all this dorky."

". . . dorky . . ."

"Dig, baby, you can stay with me if you want. My pad's just around the corner."

". . . dorky

dorky dorky dorky dorky dorky dorky dorky dorky dorky dorky dorky dorky dorky dorky dorky dorky dorky dorky . . ."

"Can we go there right now? I can't take anymore of this dorky."

". . . dorky dorky dorky dorky dorky dorky dorky . . ."

"Sure, baby, let's go."

". . . dorky . . ."

"Do you think . . . he'll be all right?"

". . . dorky dorky dorky dorky dorky dorky dorky dorky dorky dorky dorky dorky dorky dorky dorky . . ."

"Yeah, he just has to work it on out, baby, let's go . . . wait a second, baby, I think he wants to give you somethin from his satchel."

". . . dorky dorky dorky dorky dorky dorky dorky dorky dorky dorky dorky dorky dorky dorky dorky dorky dorky . . ."

"It's a music box. Do you want me to have this music box, is that it?"

". . . dorky dorky dorky dorky dorky dorky dorky . . ."

"He's tryin to tell you somethin, baby."

". . . dorky dorky dorky dorky dorky dorky . . ."

"Thank you, it's a lovely music box."

". . . dorky dorky dorky . . ."

"Come on, baby, let's go. So long, man, take it easy with your dorky."

". . . dorky dorky dorky dorky dorky dorky dorky dorky

dorky dorky. . . ."

22
Good-bye Horse Badorties' Four Pads

Dorky-day, man, has changed my life, I see that now. For now that it is the day after dorky-day, I have a clear picture of what I must do with my life. I must, man, and this is absolute necessity, move out of these four pads. The four flights of stairs are too much, man, they keep me too healthy. The time, man, has come to get out of these four pads NOW, man, right now!

"Horse Badorties, man, is making his last tape-recorded

message from East Fourth Street. I am packing it in, man, I am splitting the scene. My four pads have got to be left behind, man. And though it is true that I must leave behind for the landlord to call his own, mountains and piles of old clothes, broken rocks, salty pretzels, and other incomparable and irreplaceable articles of valuable precious design, it is necessary, man, as I am packing only my satchel. I am packing that satchel right now, man, with samples of sheet music, with tape recorders, with fans, broken clock, unforgettable pimento jar, and last of all, man, my umbrella. And now, man, it is good-bye, to my four pads."

I leave it behind me, man, stuffed to the ceilings, just as I have left other pads behind me in New Orleans, Acapulco, San Francisco, Miami Beach, Pittsburgh, and Poughkeepsie—sacred temples, man, jammed to the framework with possessions. Wherever Horse has gone, man, he has erected a pile of old laundry and tin cans, never, man, to be forgotten by the janitor, landlord, or cleaning lady who enters in thereafter to cart it all away. Piles with piles of gnarled filthiness, man, and things everywhere in indredible mixtures of color.

"So long, old pads. I'm closing the doors for the last time."

My work, my action painting, misinterpreted, is taken away and destroyed. But that's how I want it, man. I shun fame.

The astonishment, man, on the janitor's face when he is confronted by this archetypal nightmare of a Horse

Badorties junk-pile-pad with a dried-out orange peel at the center, is worth the price of admission, man. I'm taking my last and farewell look at it, man, and now I am closing the door forever, little junk pile, good-bye.

When the janitor walks in there, man, with his mop and pail and maybe an old cardboard box to sweep the dust into, he is astounded. He staggers, man, against the wall, thinking to himself, *I've seen it all now*. He is instantly illuminated, man. It's part of my work as avatar of social consciousness. Once you have tried to clean up a Horse Badorties pad, man, nothing ever troubles you again. You have had the Great Death, man.

The janitor, man, when he goes in there will lug out old ripped rugs and rags and impossible-to-analyze black grease. And then he will pass into new and still deeper frames of old trash baskets and paper bags bursting with garbage. He'll shake his head, man, and wonder. He'll tell his grandchildren about it: *I saw a pile one time. . . .*

Down the stairs, man, down the stairs, and through the hallway. There is the landlord, man, standing on the stoop, man, looking at me, and turning red in the face.

"YOU SONABITCH BASTAR'! You still here, I tol' you. . . ."

"Here are the keys, man. I've been spending the last few days cleaning up the pad, man, scrubbing down the floors and polishing the woodwork. I didn't want to leave the place looking like a wreck, man, you understand. I figured I owed you that much. All the trash has been taken out, man. I worked through the night and the Sanitation Department came around with a truck early this morning and hauled it away, maybe you saw it."

"Didn't see nothin. . . ."

"Yes, it was quite early. Anyway, it's all straightened up now, man, ready for occupancy by a little old lady. I had a chick come over and we hung a few curtains on the windows. It looks kind of nice, man, you ought to see it with the sunlight coming through."

"Yeah . . . yeah, I'll do that."

"Right, man, it'll make your day brighter. Well, so long, man. If you come across anything left behind in a cupboard or something, give it to the Merchant Marine Library. So long, man, stay cool."

And that's it, man. I'm straight with the world. I have left behind me a telephone bill of enormous complexity, man, with calls to Alaska, Hong Kong, Bombay, and the Fiji Islands. A clean get-away once more. I have only one problem, man, a minor one, and that is, where am I going to live?

Just walk along Avenue A, man, something will turn up. What is this, man, it appears to be an abandoned store with a *For Rent* sign in the window. Huge windows, man, right on street level. Look at all the room in there, man. My dorky-meter is registering an intensity of six on a scale of seven. "This is it, man! THIS IS MY NEW PAD!"

23
The Avatar at Work

"I am in my new pad, man, making the first tape in my new little home. I've given the landlord a rubber check for three hundred dollars, and now will ensue the long hassle of he and his lawyers to throw me out. But in the meantime, man, and until that happens, here we are—in the STORE! The store, more room to store things than I've ever had before. There is so much space, man, in my dark dingy store, I've got to call my printer right away and have him print up fifty thousand more sheets of music to pile up to the ceiling."

And now comes the incredible long-to-be-wondered-at Horse Badorties miracle pile-up. In what appears to be only the passing of a few moments, the time of a mere afternoon, which flickers and jumps like an underground film, I, Horse Badorties, carry in, one right after another, boxes of sheet music, scattering them around. And then going quickly back out, speeded-up to lightning-flash intensity, I drag in old broken furniture found in the street, a ripped lampshade, a piece of an armchair, a disintegrating mattress. Trip after remarkable trip is made, in a brief interlude of magnificent collecting, whereby piles of grocery bags are brought in, stuffed with shiny new cans of food and cereal boxes. And suddenly, the cans are empty and thrown around and the corn flakes are trampled into the floor, and the cleaned-up store becomes covered with greasy filth-pots, and higher and higher grows the pile, up and up, filling in all the light spaces, growing with every flickering frame, and finally, suddenly, there I am—Horse Badorties, man, standing in the middle of another piled-up-to-the-ceiling immovable blobs postcards everything, filled-up STORE!

There is hardly room to turn around. How wonderful, man.

24
Uncle Skulky

And now, man, it is time for my Love Chorus rehearsal. I am leaving the store, man, with the windows bulging out after me, and I am going up the street, man, toward St. Nancy's where the Love Chorus has gathered for a unique musical experience. Here I am again, man, going into St. Nancy's, down the aisle and up the steps, man, to the choir loft, where everyone is waiting, man, for Maestro Badorties, who must pause only briefly here on the last step for a beneficial herb-smoke, man, of Bugloss Root, to clear the Japanese beetles out of his Chinese shoes. How wonderful, man, to see my chorus again, I can hardly see them, man, my vision is going, man, the witch doctors have done it, oh no, man, wait a second, man, it is only because I am wearing my special Horse Badorties Corrective-vision Sunglasses, man, with the single peephole in the corner of one lense, man, so that you go boggle-eyed and blind from wearing them, man, how wonderful to take them off, man, and see again.

"Now, Love Chorus, it is time I introduced you to the final purification process in music. It is called Uncle Skulky and it goes like this—"

Now, man, I give them my face in three-quarter profile, in a brief tableau, man, and I roll my eyeballs into the corners of my sockets, so that I am peering at them from on high, sideways. And bringing my elbows into my chest and extending my forearms like an arthritic Polynesian dancer, I wave them, man, serpentlike and slithering. I am their insane Uncle Skulky, man, skulking through the attic, along the hallway of their minds.

This is a hideous face, man, and perhaps it is the most hideous of all my faces, man, because it is not something long-buried like my tyranosaurus-rex, but something which lived in my family tree not very long ago, man. Dear old Uncle Skulky, man, is the impossibly mad relative we all have sleeping in our souls. He would absolutely come up and claim me, man, take me over and drive me completely schizo, man, except for the fact that every now and then I take Uncle Skulky out and air him, man, let him run around and skulk a bit, after which he goes back down into his horrible secret chamber, man, and leaves me alone.

"All right, everyone, let us all take our places in the Uncle Skulky tableau."

Incredible, man, twenty-five chicks rolling their eyes into the corners of the sockets, and putting their hands into the mad-creeping position, and now all of us together are skulking across the balcony and down the winding stairway, man, where we proceed to the aisles of the church, man, and go skulking up and down them.

"Excellent, now begin, one two . . ."

Uncle Skulky sings, man, a song of weirdness unrivalled. Skulking past the flickering candles of the altar, we sing our Uncle Skulky music, man, making faces so fiendish and weird that any last inhibitions the chicks have about music is now being erased completely. We are totally cleansed, man. We have lived out the worst thing in us. From tyranosaurus-rex to Uncle Skulky to NBC, man, we are on the way. The Love Chorus has learned how to sing together, man!

25
The Fan Man Eats It

It is nighttime on the Lower East Side, man, and having worked all day filling up my store, and all night singing Uncle Skulky, I am now having a piña-colada at a lunch counter, imbibing healthy vitality and digestive enzymes to digest the total emptiness of my stomach. How I wish, man, I had a dirty hot dog.

Wandering around, man, stumbling around hungrily through the Lower East Side night, searching for the ultimate hot dog. I'd better have a pizza instead with mushrooms. Wait a second, man, here is a place frying up sausages with onions and peppers, man, look at all those juicy pig intestines, man, crackling and bubbling there, stuffed with ground-up fecal matter and eyeballs, I think instead, man, I'll go along here a little further, to a nice clean quiet restaurant, man, and order a cheese sandwich . . . wait a second, man, I HAVE IT! I will go to the macrobiotic restaurant for a plate of brown rice, with shredded apron in it, and perhaps some old dishrag tea. It's a fact, man, I know a chick who worked there, and she told me she actually discovered one day, an old rag in the great Zen teapot.

Maybe I won't go there after all, man. I could have instead, if I simply walk along here fourteen or fifteen blocks to the disgusting West Village, a Greek sandwich, stuffed with chick-peas and onions and sesame paste, called filafel, man, and if I eat one of them I'll feel awful. No, man, I'd better think of something else. I've got it, man, I'll just turn southeast here, turn completely around and walk back along Second Avenue, man, to the INDIAN RESTAURANT, man! That's it. Have spicy hot vegetable curry, flaming tumeric coriander mustard powder cayenne pepper, inflame my stomach, make my eyes water, I'll be farting firecrackers, man, I'd better not.

Relax, man, there is a simple enough answer. You'll simply ride uptown on the subway to Fortieth Street, to the Blarney Stone bar, and have some home-fried potatoes and a glass of beer. And several slices of roast beef, running red with blood and probably kill me.

No, man, hold everything and start walking directly to the West Village again, to the health-food bar for a drink of carrot juice. Man, why didn't I think of it sooner? A delicious cool orange-colored drink of vitamin A juicy carrot which will turn my skin orange and make me look weird on television. Cancel the carrot juice, man.

Instead I'll have a plain old vegetarian cutlet at the dairy restaurant right down the block here, man, on Second Avenue once again, a vegetable cutlet, man, so heavy you think you've eaten sixteen hamburgers.

THAT'S IT, MAN! Sixteen hamburgers with onions on them, to go! Definitely, man, Forty-second Street, get out your token, we're riding.

No, an onion roll from Yonaschimmel's down on Delancy Street is closer, man, a hot freshly-baked onion roll. Impossible, man, I just remember Buddha advises against onions, they asphyxiate the thousand little gods of the body.

This is an existential crisis, man. My back is against the wall. I'm starving, man, and cannot find the perfect food. My all-important Love Concert is in just two more days. I must without further consideration go directly back to this lunch counter, man, and have another piña-colada, continuing my liquid diet.

"Piña-colada, man."

"All gone, man, de piña-colada ees dry."

"Good, man, I didn't want one anyway. I'd better have

a dish of . . . wait a . . . just a . . . see you later, man . . . I have to. . . ."

Think it over, man. If this continues, man, I will still be walking the streets tomorrow morning at sunrise, looking for a hot dog. I'll just buy a candy bar, that's all, man, fuck it. No, man, candy sugar causes juvenile delinquency, don't you read your issue of the *Weekly Compost Heap*?

Walking along, man, working out the perfect diet. Old Chinese sages, man, lived on saliva. The perfect food. Only requirement is that you spend your entire life lying down, doing absolutely nothing. The Way Of Heaven. That's it, man, that's the diet for me.

I now know what I must do, man. I will fast tonight, and tomorrow night being the final rehearsal for the Love Concert, I will spend the entire day tomorrow in Van Cortlandt Park, eating leaves and berries and the roots of thistle bushes. I will soak up the energy of my childhood, man, and it will give me tremendous vitality for the concert on the following day. That is the program. It is sane, it is clear, it is efficient, it receives inner confirmation on my dorky-meter. My entire being responds to this suggestion, with a feeling of peace and contentment. Therefore, having solved the dilemma in a manner befitting an artist of my stature, I am going directly back to my store, to turn in for a sleep. Calmly and coolly with my entire personality reverberating, I will leave early in the morning on the subway for Van Cortlandt Park, and engage in vital meditation and nibbling shrubbery. Perhaps I will even take along a can of Beeferoni and cook it up on a fire in the woods, made in a little place of rocks. What a wonderful and well-reasoned program this is, Horse Badorties. You should be a college professor.

26 Something Calls to the Fan Man, Faintly

It is morning, Horse Badorties, what a wonderful sunshining morning, wait a second, man, it is afternoon, I overslept. I must hurry, man, if I am to get up to Van Cortlandt Park and back down again for the last rehearsal before the great Horse Badorties Love Chorus Concert. Don't fuck around in your trash pile, man, just grab your satchel and umbrella and screw out of the store.

OK, man, I am going straight out the door, without

breakfast, without looking around, without fucking off, without looking over my piles of stuff. I am in the actual sunlight of the street already, man, closing my store, and walking along. Man, I must be straightening out my life, if I am able to leave my store-pad so easily. I must be shaping up, man, becoming a superman, man!

Have I forgotten anything?

Sunglasses, tape recorder, fan, umbrella, satchel . . . it looks like I have everything I need, man, for a day in wonderful Van Cortlandt Park. It is finally happening, man. My life is coming together in coordinated units.

Getting on the subway, man, and riding, riding, up the long lonely tunnel, man, back to my childhood.

Riding, riding, tunnel lights flashing past. A solitary Horse Badorties am I, carrying satchel and holding gigantic umbrella, on the way to the trees and paths of Van Cortlandt Park. And tomorrow night, man, I will conduct the Love Chorus before the eyes of the world. A great new day is dawning for you, Horse Badorties, filled with fans and . . .

. . . we're coming up out of the underground tunnel, man, the subway train is rising up on the old familiar stilts, climbing the elevated framework, and there, sprawling out below me, man, is the Bronx. I must take a picture of this view, man, through the window, with my Japanese superplastic camera, man. I bought the entire kit, with little plastic developing tank and trays and fluid. It is so wonderful, man, to take pictures and then develop them and see floating up before my eyes in the stop bath, nothing at all, man, just black shadows, maybe, and a little spray of faint streaks.

Shaking back and forth subway car, maybe fall over, topple down onto street. There, man, down there was where I used to live . . . no, wait a second, man, it's up further.

You're wrong, man, this IS the stop, quick, man, hold the door the phone . . .

. . . here I am, man, on the platform in the Bronx. Everything is clicking, man, everything is going off smoothly. And now, man, it is down the steps and up the street and directly into mystical, magical Van Cortlandt Park, man, which stretches on out for many miles of secret trails.

Walking along through green trees and then upwards, man, getting higher, higher. Standing on a plateau, man, at the edge of the park, looking down at the distant buildings. I am Merlin, man. The mystery of the old park is mine to contemplate again. What a wonderful idea to come here, man, on the day before the Love Concert. The primal surge of childhood. I used to wander here, man, a spaced-out little Horse Badorties.

Coming into a meadow, man, leaving all sight of buildings behind. Pastoral mood, going into the high grass with satchel and umbrella, the wandering Knight of the Hot Dog pauses for a smoke.

All time is mine, man. What time is it, man, by the large alarm clock in my satchel? It is four o'clock, man, plenty of time before rehearsal, time to wind on, and go down this mysterious tunnel that only rabbits, mad hatters, and Horse Badorties know. Carrying mad satchel, going down, under the highway, and entering further into the park, man, on the lost muddy trails of youth. No threat from the environment, down through here, there is a little swamp, with birds and frogs. Dreams, man, all long-lost dreams awakening again.

Jesus, man, here it is, here is the very tree against which I laid my first chick . . . no, wait a second, man, it was this one over here. Here it is, man, I had the wrong tree.

There's the golf course, man, guys driving little balls, and I am driving my dream on out over time.

Here, man, are the old railroad tracks that run through the park, and here, man, is where I am going to slip down into the bushes and relax, man. The sun is on me, and this, man, is my long-awaited day. Tomorrow afternoon about this time, man, I will become a public artist.

"Where's Horse, man?"

"I don't know, man, don't worry, he's always late."

"Have you fellows seen Horse?"

"No, Father."

"Well, his fans arrived at the church this morning. We might as well take them over to Tompkins Square. I suppose he's probably there already."

"I'll try to get him on the walkie-talkie, Father. . . .

Hello, man . . . hello, Horse . . . can you hear me, man. . . ? it's concert time, man, where are you?"

"All right, everyone, let's go now, over to the park."

"Horse, man, come in, man . . . we are leaving the church, man, and are heading up the street toward the Square. Where are you, man? Come quick, over."

Yes, man, this is the life of my childhood, laying up here in Van Cortlandt Park by the railroad tracks, dreaming deep into my ancient feelings, man. Different lifetimes gathering around, and I go in and out, man, of ever-widening bands of sensitive awareness. What a wonderful day in the park, man. This is just the preparation I need for my debut tomorrow afternoon. This, man, was one of your best ideas. It shows improvement of character and development of will power.

"Hello, Horse, come in, man. We are walkin into Tompkins Square, man, and NBC is here, man. Big vans, man, and cameras and tape machines and cables all over the fuckin place. There's a huge audience, man, all kinds of people, man. We'll stall them off, man, hurry on and get here, over."

I was a Chinese cat once, man, I'm certain of this as I sit here by these railroad tracks. I can't forget a thing like that, man. My memory, man, is composed of perfectly integrated forms. I have the missing centuries in my grip, man, brought back into consciousness through musical discipline. I've studied it all, man, I know the music of the ages. A memory like this is a great power, man, to be used for the good of the world. I will have to open a special Memory School, man, and train people to remember all of their lifetimes, or money back.

"Hello, Horse, man . . . please, man, where are you. . . ? I can't hold them off any longer, man. The NBC director is gettin nervous, man, over. . . ."

"You can't reach him, Frank?"

"No, Father, he's out of walkie-talkie range."

"Well, I suppose we shall just have to sing without him. It will be difficult without a conductor, won't it?"

"I guess I can conduct it, Father."

"What about those neighborhood boys playing drums at the foot of the bandstand?"

"I'll have to ask them to knock it off." Puerto Rican drummers, man, wailin on the conga, the bongo drums. Go over, man, and tell them to knock it off, get my head knocked off. Horse, man, where are you? "Hey, man, how about shuttin down your drums for awhile, man, so we can sing?"

BUM BUMP BUM BUM BUM
BUM BUMP BUMP BUM BUM

"You dig, man, we got a show, man, to do, sing a couple songs, man, it won't take long, how about givin us a break, man?"

ROCK-A-TOCKA-TOCKA-TOCKA-ROCKA
BUM BUMP BUM BUM BUM

Horse Badorties remembers, man, he remembers sweet and innocent childhood here in the park. When I was a little kid, man, I used to see strange thing in my head, man. Used to see guys in turbans, chanting. And Chinese cats, man, playing flute. And a mountain, man, in Tibet, where they were blowing twenty-foot horns, man. I came into this world, man, remembering where I'd been. And that is why, man, the Love Concert is so important to me, man, because of all the music I have ever done, man, in a thousand million lifetimes, it is the most beautiful. Tomorrow afternoon, man, the world will hear what it has not heard for five hundred years, man, and it will then REMEMBER! Yes, man, all those lifetimes. Which one have I left out, man? Something seems to be calling me from afar.

RICK-TICKA-TICKA-TOCK
BUM BUMP BUM BUM

"Look, man, if you'll just knock it off, man, for a few minutes till I get the singers lined up, man, we can do this fuckin concert together, man. You can do the rhythm in the background, man, drum it along with us, whattya say, man? We'll work it out together."

"OK, mon. *Hombres, silencio*!"

"Cool, man, that's great. When I'm set up there on the stage, man, I'll give you the downbeat, and you and the boys come in soft, man, dig?"

"I deeg, mon. Me and de boys play you some drum."

"Alright, chorus on stage. Here are your fans, everyone. Take one from the box."

"Do we have to hold these fans, Frank?"

"Look, baby, that's how Horse wanted it, man, and that's how he'll get it. Everybody hold their fan up in one hand, that's it, point it at your face. Everybody's fan workin? All right, sing with the little note of the fan and we'll all be pitched together. Hey, NBC, man, we're ready, man."

"CUE ANNOUNCE."

"A single moment of prayer, Frank?"

"Right, Father." Where are you, Horse, you motherfucker, I never directed no chorus before, man, and my hand is shakin.

Yes, man, I, Horse Badorties, abominable footprint and freak, have for the first time in my life neatly arranged and carefully executed Master Plan A. With one more solid night of rehearsal, man, Love Chorus will be ready. My mission, man, the mission for which I came back to

Earth, man, is nearing completion. I'm rising up from the railroad bank, man, and I am walking through the trees, a whole person, at last.

"OK, here we go everyone . . . one two three and. . . ." Perfect, man, everybody together, now man, just keep them rollin along like Horse does, man, wavin your arms like a big bird, man, bring in the drums, man, and . . .

. . . NOW . . .

Now, hombres, le's hob de drum, das eet, ni' and soft.

OK, man, there are the drums, they roll by themselves, man, island drums, man, in the background, right in the groove. And way out behind me, man, I can hear the cameras grindin. Together, we are together, man, the chords are sweet the way Horse likes them, and strong, risin up through the trees, man, out over the park and I am flappin my wings, man, takin off into the sky, lookin for Horse, man, where are you, man?

"Horse Badorties here, making a tape-recorded message in Van Cortlandt Park. I finally got here, man, to the scene of yesteryear. It is official now, man. On the day before the Lower East Side Love Concert, Horse Badorties dragged his valuable precious person to the Bronx, to have mystic visions in preparation for the Big Night, tomorrow. Years from now, man, I will hear this tape and the concert will already be over and past. It's a strange thought, man."

The Love Chorus, man. I have that music in my heart. I can hear it right now, in my inner ear, man. Secret magic music, man, artistically perfect. I am happy, man, to be able to bring this music to the world tomorrow. And now, man, in the fading afternoon light, I am going to make a little fire in the woods, man, and cook up this can of vegetarian steaks, man, so that I may be strong for the performance. This will be my last meal before the crucial hour. I will go into the Love Concert light as a Chinese saliva sage.

We are singin it perfect, man, the chicks, Father, me, and the PR drummers, man, it's real, man, it is workin out, now, to the end, man, keep them all harmonic, don't nobody fall off the notes, man. The chicks, man, their hair is blowin out, risin gently from the breezes of the fans, man. Horse's fans, man, keep you cool and in the music. That's all, that's it, now, now, now, risin UP, in strong with the drums, roll, roll, hold that note soprano bass tenor alto hold it, let it shimmer and shine up there in the evenin air, in the trees, in the quiet. Man, my guts are jumpin, man, this conductin give you an ulcer, man, I got to get back to the sax, just a little more, everyone, so we can touch the cloud, man, and that's all!

Silencio!

"Camera two, close in there, at the bandstand, and get some of those faces."

Kids runnin around, a dog takin a piss on a tree, all kinds of stoned people, smilin, man, we did it!

Walking through the trees out here in Van Cortlandt Park, man, at evening. Christ, man, am I seeing things? I am seeing the most incredible sight, man, of my life. Puerto Rican kids, man, in green uniforms and black berets, man, coming through the trees and bushes of Van Cortlandt Park, man, carrying toy guns and hand grenades, man, maybe not toys give you a blast with it, blow me to Yankee Stadium. Puerto Rican kids, man, armed, in platoon formation, training in the woods. For what, man, are they training?

Through the bushes, man, about fifty of them. And here comes their leader, man, a snappy-looking sonofabitch, man, with G.I. outfit, white spats, spiffy uniform. I wonder, man, would he want to buy a fan?

"Hey, man, you need one of these fans, man. Dig, Corporal, a breeze to blow the dust off your medals. Look, man, you just press the button . . . wait a second, man, it's jammed, I have to shake the water out of it. . . ."

"To the right flank, HO!"

"Ho is right, man. Ho Chi Minh had one, man, and you should have one too. A buck-ninety-five, man, with batteries."

"One, two, hut, two. . . ."

Right on through the bushes, man. The cat doesn't need a fan, man. He's cool already. He has his own army. Pretty soon, man, the mayor will be pulling piña-colada in a little white hat on One-Hundred-First Street and Amsterdam Avenue, man. You watch, man. The Puerto Ricans, man. Taking over, man. It's coming, man. Any day now. RUN TO THE HILLS, MAN!

"Alright, gentlemen, pack it up. Roll in those cables. Great show, Father. The kids sang beautifully. How'd you get them into line?"

"By making dinosaur faces."

"OK, *hombres*, let's hob some more drum!"

BUM BUMP BUM BUM BUM

BUM BUMP BUM BUMP BUM

"Hello, Horse, hello, man, can you read me, man. The concert came off OK, man, wherever you are."

I'm passing through bushes, man, into the great open soccer field of Van Cortlandt Park, man, where the Puerto Rican soccer players are kicking the ball around, somebody's head maybe, and the sky, man, is cloudy, and a gentle wind is blowing up. I'm coming out into the big green expanse of lawn, man, and am heading back toward the subway. I have circled the park, man, picking up vital energies from the earth of my childhood, man, and I am prepared for a tremendously sensitive rehearsal, man, in which I will pull together the last little delicate subtle modalities of the world's greatest music.

And dig, man, I feel a raindrop.

"This is Horse Badorties, man, making a specially recorded weather report on tape, man. It is raining, man, at last. I have been carrying this gigantically heavy umbrella around for weeks, man, day in and day out, and now the time has come, man, TO OPEN IT!"

Opening the great Hot Dog Umbrella, man, pushing up the ribs along the centerpole and spreading it out over my head, man, in a tremendous expanse of red white and blue cloth.

"It is up, man. It is up and over my head. Listen, man, to the raindrops beating down on it. The soccer players are running for cover, man, in the bushes, but I'm covered already, man. I am slowly heading across the huge green lawn toward the subway, man, satchel in one hand, umbrella in the other, stepping through puddles. Everything is cool, man, beneath the great umbrella. Horse Badorties is ready for the monsoon."

AUTHOR PHOTO © ANNIE LEIBOVITZ
COVER DESIGN © JOHN SPOSATO

Obelisk